Monkey Wrench

John L. Thompson

Books by
John L. Thompson

Truck Stop Trilogy
-Truck Stop
-Monkey Wrench
-Dead Blow (Sep, 2021)

Short Story Collections

Dimensional Ruins: Humanities End

Books Edited for
Dead Guns Press

Hardboiled: Crime and Detective
Hardboiled: Crime Scene
Hardboiled: Dames and Sin
Hardboiled
Badlands
Undead War
Hangmen and Bullets

ISBN **978-1-7324281-3-3**

Cover Design by Dusty Desert Press

Monkey Wrench

John L. Thompson

A Dusty Desert Press Publication

For those who didn't have a chance for the first story…

Don't throw a monkey-wrench into the machinery.

– Philander Chase Johnson

You may have to fight a battle more than once to win it.

– Margaret Thatcher

A man cannot be comfortable without his own approval.

–Mark Twain

ONE

OCTOBER, 2008

The cold wind whipped against my face, forcing a hard shiver up my spine. The Mossberg 500 twelve-gauge only added to the misery with its frozen steel seeping through my hand. I cursed and flipped up the collar on my jacket hoping to ward off the worst of it. I kept a wary eye on the swaying trees and the ever-shifting shadows. Branches smashed and raked against each other as if tossing out a warning. We were in bad guy territory. Dixie Mafia territory.

Or was it the ghosts of Dave Musgrave and Lonnie Blonde?

I scanned the shadows. The dark lands were drenched in their blood and shivered in protest. Someone or anyone from the Dixie Mafia might be out there. I checked that the safety was off on the Mossberg. I figured if anyone from the Dixie Mafia was watching from the shadows it had to be the enforcers' Cleeve and Robert Lee, maybe even Thomas Hauser. I had my suspicions they had done in Musgrave. Never mind he was a devout Dixie Mafia member. He crossed the line somewhere and got whacked for it. I suspected he was murdered over the money. The same money Logan and I had been looking for the past year.

It all starts with rumors. Every truck stop in the world is loaded with them. Anyone listening long enough can only believe in pieces of the quarter-truths and halved-falsehoods. After a while, you start putting the real story together. Duggan's Truck Stop was no exception. The truth of the rumors was Duggan's franchise was a front for the Dixie Mafia, a mob group based out of Biloxi, Mississippi. Everyone working there had a kind of idea of the rumor being true. No one wanted to believe it but no one was saying it was false either.

It was around 2006 before the rumor train started moving through Duggan's about a lot of money going missing. The Biloxi boys had caught on and the word was they wanted it back. No one was sure about the amount. Was it a million? A few bucks and pennies? No one knew but it was missing. New faces prowled the complex. Some of these were hard-core critters from Mississippi. I figured it was a substantial amount to justify those new faces. That included Cleeve and Robert Lee, twins with more muscle than brains.

At the centre of the controversy? Dave Musgrave and Lonnie Blonde...

Dave Musgrave was the shop manager. He was hooked up with Lonnie Blonde the bookkeeper. It was easy enough for her to snip off a few bucks from the money tree every now and then. I knew him for about three, almost four years. He was tied up in some shady shit. Everyone knew it but turned a blind eye to it. Besides pushing guns and dope through the shop, he kept tabs on the whores working the lot servicing truck drivers. He was tied to the Dixie Mafia hard-core.

Then, one night, Dave Musgrave and Lonnie Blonde caught an acute case of lead poisoning right here on his property. The secret to the whereabouts of the location of the money went with Musgrave and Lonnie Blonde on board the Hell's Express.

Everybody, including the Feds, was looking for the legendary Musgrave fortune he had buried out here on his ranch. All of them had failed, but now, Logan and I, a couple of diesel mechanics, might just have out-smarted all of them. All our searching, researching, had led us to this moment.

I was sure of it.

I looked down at the dark hole in the ground. A large metal plate was propped up on several pieces of steel rebar. The entrance led down to a buried conex. Musgrave had buried his fortune down there.

A head popped up out of the ground. Logan held up an old .50 caliber ammo can. "Hendricks!"

I frowned. Logan was a big risk. He was busy banging Amy Hauser. A bad move on his part. I tried warning him. Amy was married to Thomas Hauser. Logan wasn't listening. I guess the sex was too damn good. With that aspect and us being out here looking for Musgraves' buried fortune the current events were ripe for disaster.

It wasn't my business to get involved on that end of things. But it sure as hell could get us all killed.

I dug around my jacket pocket, gripped the flashlight, and flashed the beam on what he held out. The ammo can was packed with Benjamin Franklins. They all wore an expression protesting the bitter cold. *Or were they lamenting the fact we had found the mob cache?* "Jesus..."

"We did it!" Logan smiled.

I clicked the light off and shifted the shotgun over to my weak hand. The clouds were hanging low. Little sparks of snow began to fall. In another hour, the area was going to get blasted with the white stuff. "C'mon, we gotta haul ass! How many?"

"Looks like nine ammo cans! All packed with cash! Hundreds and fifties!"

"Bring 'em up," I snarled. "C'mon! Let's go!"

Logan disappeared. I checked the shadows all around, hoping no one was out there. This was the moment of truth. If the Dixie boys were lying in wait, now would be the time to hit us.

Logan grunted and began handing up the ammo cans. I reached down, grabbing them while trying to maintain a grip on the Mossberg, and keeping a wary eye on the ever-shifting shadows.

When the last can was handed up, Logan scrambled out of the hole. I held up the plate with another longer piece of rebar while Logan kicked away the props. I let the plate fall back in place. A large burst of dust exploded in the air. Scrambling, I found an old branch and swept the area over before tossing a bunch of dead branches and debris over the spot. Logan strapped up the ammo cans with a section of nylon rope he'd bought with him.

Satisfied with my handiwork, we took up our bundles and moved away down the hill. We carefully navigated through the bush and over the clusters of slick sandstone rocks. We stopped once when we were fifty yards or so from the truck. I knelt, watched, and listened. Only the sounds of the winds and shivering trees could be heard. I signaled to move out and we approached Logan's Ford with caution.

We were reading each other. No point in being sloppy now. I shot a look behind us and raised the Mossberg to my shoulder. I popped the door open, but all that met us was the rotten thread-bare bench seat. I set the ammo cans down in the back of the bed. Logan fired off the Ford and then began cramming the ammo cans inside the tool storage box in the back of the bed. I kept the Mossberg's barrel pointed out across the dark lands.

Nothing.

No one.

Are we going to make it?

We jumped in the Ford. Logan threw it in gear and began rolling, but left the headlights off. He gripped his .45 hard in one hand and steered with the other. I looked behind us, half-expecting headlights to flare to life, but nothing.

Logan steered the Ford down one path, shifted over onto another leading out of the Dunes, and back to the asphalt road. Logan sped up, hit the asphalt at fifty. The rear wheels slipped before regaining traction.

The snow picked up in tempo. It was falling hard enough that the wipers were having trouble slapping away the large blotches of splattered snow. Within hours the snow would cover up the lands in a thick blanket. No one would ever know we had found the money. It was clear sailing from here.

I looked over to Logan. The grip on his .45 was relaxed. I smiled. His face cracked open into a soft laugh. I began slapping the dash. The tension erupted into howls of laughter and fist-pumping. God damn, we've done it! We pulled off a perfect caper. We found the money.. We outsmarted the Feds, the Dixie Mafia, and everyone else looking for the cache.

All we had to do was stay quiet...run silent, run deep.

TWO

MAY, 2009

Of course, being silent can be a difficult thing to accomplish. The thing about the Dixie Mafia is that they don't forget, and they have plenty of time to figure out if you shafted them in the ass. There's always a day of retribution and consequence. I just didn't realize it would come around so soon. No matter how hard we tried to stay silent and live normal, somewhere along the line, the Dixie boys figured it all out.

I kicked the window out on the camper. The mangled glass panel tumbled out into the dark. I slid out over the frame. The jagged glass fragments stuck in the remaining framework, raked across my back tearing into my flesh. I hit the ground and took off running into the dark prairie land. Behind me, the camper shook violently. A man screamed in agony.

A baseball bat to the nuts will usually generate that kinda reaction.

I had maybe a few seconds before the trio of Dixie Mafia guys came running. I went into a full sprint. I got about fifty yards easy, looked back over my shoulder. Cleeve staggered out of the camper. He was holding his crotch and cursing out loud. The thing that grabbed my attention was the large-frame revolver he was holding.

He lifted it.

I veered left and picked up speed, praying the dark void of the evening would shield me. I had a small chance to escape. An old irrigation ditch lay a mere hundred yards off. The ditch hadn't been used in decades. God only knew what was down there but it beat the alternative.

Another look back.

Two more shadows emerged from around the corner of the camper. I knew who they were. Thomas and Robert Lee began blasting their hand cannons adding to the confusion. Explosions thundered across the valley. The heavy bullets buzzed overhead. One smacked the ground, a larger burst of dirt exploding up into the air. Then, more shouts of rage and frustration. I made the tangled cluster of elms growing along the ditch bank edges. More shots rang out, the bullets tumbling through the branches swaying in protest.

I lost my footing, tripped, and fell in a long arc before impacting face-first at the bottom of the ditch. Within the explosion of stars, my jaw popped. I rolled around in agony within the thick overgrown vegetation within the ditch. I hit a patch of prickly pear and let out a yelp. It was enough to bring me around. I gathered up the remaining bits of wits I had in reserve, forced myself up, and bolted deeper into the thick brush.

The sounds of heavy feet pounding the earth drew closer. My heart hammered against my rib cage. Adrenaline pulsed through my veins like lightning strikes. I scrambled off deeper into a thick patch of dense prairie grass and thorn bush. The tangled branches of Chinese elms overhead grabbed and tore my shirt. Thorn bushes made small cuts across my skin but I pressed deeper into the thicket. I collapsed behind a thick stump of elm, wheezing and gagging. I reached up with a trembling hand, took hold of my shoulder, plucking and brushing at the cactus spines sticking out of the fabric of the black t-shirt.

I froze.

Beams of light cut through the night. Thomas's voice bellowed in rage.

"You fucking imbecile," Thomas yelled. "You had one fucking job!"

"He hit my nuts with a bat!" Cleeve protested.

The light flashed, moving down the ditch and up the sides.

Robert Lee snickered. "You let him nail your nuts?"

"Shut up, Robert!" Cleeve groaned.

"Were you two getting all pretty in there or something?" Robert Lee laughed.

"The two of you just shut the hell up!" Thomas shouted. He stabbed the light on the two men. "You think this is a game?"

Silence. Cleeve was still massaging his balls.

"We got the money. We got one chance to get the guns. Let's go get that whore wife of mine and her fuck boy."

"Thomas?" Robert Lee asked. "What about Hendricks?"

The light flashed back down the ditch, sweeping from side to side. "We lost him," he swore. "He'll show up eventually," a brief silence and then with hate dripping from his tone. "And we'll deal with it then. Right now? We have other loose ends. Let's move."

"Uncle going to be mad," whined Cleeve.

"And you think I ain't?" Thomas shoved Cleeve away from the ditch edge. "Let's go!"

The sound of footfalls brushing through the prairie grass faded. I clawed back up the ditch bank, reaching the rim. I poked my head up just high enough to see what the trio was doing. They were tearing apart the camper. That was expected. Cursing, I began doubting going after the money in the first place. It was worse thinking I had stashed my portion of it in the kitchen cabinet. I did have the backup plan: I'd stashed ten grand in the well-house. I should've crammed the whole thing down there. I swore, pounding my forehead against the ground.

The bulky shadow of Thomas came out of the camper. He was holding an old gym bag. I knew what it was. The money was no longer mine, and there were going to be repercussions.

THREE

I laid there in the bush, watching the goons rip my camper apart. A breeze rattled the limbs on the surrounding trees. The cool earth felt good against the bangs and bruises I'd gotten from Cleeve. It shocked the hell out of me when the camper door flew open and Cleeve stormed in and proceeded to beat my ass. I was lucky to get my grubby hands on the ball bat.

I started thinking the money was just a cursed deal from the start. I should've left months ago. I should've just packed up Jill along with everything else and shagged ass in the middle of the night. I looked up to the dark skies, cursing my lot in life to God above. The window of opportunity had been wide open then.

I cursed the name of Logan Pierce and Amy Hauser.

I cursed everything associated with the half-million cash pile found in that God-damned conex box buried deep underground.

I should've said to hell with Logan and Amy. What they did was their business, not mine.

But...

I was just as equally to blame.

Robert Lee stepped out of the camper, tossed my flat screen to the ground. A few stomps and the plastic casing shattered. I mumbled a curse. If I had a rifle, I would've shot the bastard in the face. I really loved that TV.

The lights in the camper died. Several minutes drifted by. I couldn't see the men but heard voices. They were leaving, or at least I hoped they were. Once they left, I'd slip in, grab a few things then, haul ass to the hills. The cell phone would be the first thing to grab. Logan had to know the storms of wrath from the Dixie Mafia were coming his way. After that, I'd run off in the Chevy. All I had to do...

A barrage of gunfire. I ducked, expecting the rounds to come flying in my direction but there were no sounds of impacts anywhere near me. I rose, shaking, numb, waiting for the inevitable death. But it never came anywhere close. Illuminated in quick flashes, the truck was being murdered. I swore. First, the tires wheezed then the sounds of leaking water splashing the earth. There was no way my truck survived the barrage.

The sounds of night returned. After long minutes had passed, the distant sound of another truck fired off further down the trail leading up to my ruined abode. I pulled myself up over the ditch bank just as the dull red glow from tail lights spun around in the dark dust and sped off.

I kept a low crouch trot back to the camper. When I got within twenty-five yards, I knelt and listened for anything out of the ordinary. Cleeve or Robert Lee might be waiting, hiding somewhere, hoping I would return. But there wasn't a sound. I moved forward again, did a quick poke and peek.

Nothing.

I fumbled for the light switch just inside the door. It hummed to life flickering from a dead element. The trailer was ransacked. I shouldn't have expected anything less. The walls were busted up. The cabinets smashed and ripped off the walls. Everything I owned was tossed to the floor. The floors were wet from a broken water line somewhere. I made a quick search for the cell phone but gave up after a while. I was resigned to the fact either they had taken it, or it was lost forever in the stew of carnage swirling around my feet.

I scratched the stubble on my chin.

The first rule of survival is to make a plan to back up the main plan. Months ago, I opted for the just-in-case-things-turned-to-shit plan. I buried ten grand at the bottom of the well house.

I jumped out and started moving to the well house but froze.

Time was not on my side. Flashing lights off Highway 41 caught my attention. I swore. Any minute, the cops were going to be here. I counted about eight sets of lights. One of the damned neighbours must've complained about all the gunfire. Not having any time to spare, I jumped back inside, grabbing up anything important. I kissed the packet of my old life, my DD-214, divorce decree, social cards, everything. I was just thankful the bastards left me those items. Taking all the papers and a few old shirts and trousers, I crammed everything in my old duffle bag and scrambled out the door. I took off across the dark lands.

Looking back, I let off a string of curses. I had to hit the road and run like hell. The flashing lights shifted direction. They were moving up Ice Plant Road. They'd be on top of me in a few minutes if I didn't move my ass into high gear. I went into a jogging run.

Maybe another time, I thought. There wasn't much else I could do. The majority of the money was gone. The Chevy was shot to pieces, the trailer wrecked, and there was no way to call anyone. I knew Logan was in deep shit but there wasn't a damn thing I could do about it. I just hoped he and Amy had enough smarts to be anywhere other than where they were at.

SHIT…

I cursed through gritted teeth and busted lips.

FOUR

There's somebody out there...

...waiting...

...someone wants to do bad things.

I looked left, then right, then back at the large glass doors. The early summer heat washed through as they slid open and then closed clamping off the warm blast. An older woman walked out, eyes straight but she wore a mask of annoyance with Jill and me standing in her way.

I stopped just before exiting, clutching the bag with a six-pack of beer and the fifth of Crown Royal. The parking lot looked harmless but there was danger lurking out there, I could feel it. Coming to Walmart was a bad idea but alcohol had always been the demon bitch perched on my shoulders. I cursed softly. Jill had an old Model 10 .38.

It belonged to her grandfather during the war. It was the only gun I had access to. I'd left it on top of the refrigerator. Jill said it made her uncomfortable like something bad was going to happen. I should've ignored her and bought it anyway.

My attention went back to the glass door. It opened again. The heat drifted in, vanquished the cool air before clamping shut again. I looked for anything out of place in the vast parking lot. A few people were strolling in and out through the sliding doors, several kids talking near a parked Honda Civic in the front row, a Walmart employee pushing a long line of baskets back toward the store, no cops, no Feds, no Dixie Mafia bad guys, no nothing. It was just another normal Sunday afternoon where people were playing hunter-gatherer at their local Walmart.

My gut was telling me something different.

"James...is everything alright?" Jill asked. There was trouble etched in her baby blues.

"I thought I saw something," I mumbled still searching for the one thing that looked out of place.

She followed my gaze, searching but couldn't see anything. "I think you're being paranoid."

"I have a right to be paranoid, don't you think?" I whispered.

"Baby, I'm seriously not seeing anything," she replied.

"They're out there."

"Who?"

"I don't know, the Dixie Mafia, the Feds, cops, take your pick."

"I think..." She started to say something but stopped.

"We've had this discussion," I said cutting her off.

"I think it should stay open as an option," The tone of her response was a low whisper tinged with fear.

"No more," I held up a hand. I didn't want to talk about it anymore.

She turned, facing me. The door slid open and a warm breeze picked up, jostling the ends of her red hair. "James, please, there is nothing out there."

I wished to hell I hadn't gone after the money. Life would be so easy about now. The bruises on my cheek and arms, gifts from the Dixie Mafia throbbed still but were fading.

I was lucky to be alive at this point.

I should never have bought Jill the new Dodge Durango. One of the tipping points in being discovered. It sat a few cars down from where the three kids were talking around the Honda, the sun glaring off the red paint job.

I looked at Jill. Her face was ghostly white, not unusual for red-heads but it was abnormal like the blood had drained from her face. "Okay, if you say there is nothing out there, then there is nothing out there."

"We'll be fine, James," she replied with a weak smile.

We went through the sliding door, into the glaring sun and were halfway across the cross-walk when I heard the sound of guns clearing leather and the screaming started. The three kids by the Honda turned out to be three men, holding up Glock pistols. From a nearby minivan, a small army of men spilled out from its sides. They held up an array of pistols and shotguns. But the striking feature was the US Marshals insignia in bright yellow scrawled across their vests. They were screaming orders. We stood frozen to the hot asphalt.

Jill gripped my hand tight, frozen in fear, a deep gasp. My first instinct was to run, dragging her by her delicate hand but every shadow cut off any chance of success. I knew the gig was up. Each gun threatened to send our immortal souls to the Lands Beyond if we tried. Several more cops materialized from the shadows and then from behind, holding up guns and screaming for me to surrender. Lights flared to life and a news crew aimed their lethal camera at us.

It was over in a matter of seconds. No matter how much I thought I might like to run, I knew from the beginning of this mess from day one it was going to be a fruitless effort. I made it for two weeks. I guess I should count myself lucky.

I leaned in and kissed Jill. I let go of her hand and held up my hands still holding the bag of beer and Crown in the hook of my fingers. Firm hands grabbed my shirt and arms, a quick, violent jerk, and I was slammed to the asphalt. The sunglasses flew off my face, and a salty finger grazed the eye. The bag of beer flew from loose fingers. The package smashed on the black, hot asphalt. White foam spilled from the plastic bag. *A shame*, I thought, *such a waste of good beer.*

A dog-pile of Marshals clamored over me, twisting my arms into impossible positions. I wasn't too kosher on the idea of being roughed up since I'd surrendered peacefully but cops are the same all over. They'll beat your ass regardless if you go peacefully or violently. I think that's why so many guys take off running. They know they're going to get an ass-beating anyways and might as well make it worthwhile.

Shit.

My mind was going twenty thousand different directions with nowhere to go. There was nothing to do about it now. Everything slowed down to fractions of a second. My breathing slowed, the world slowed. I was hoisted up to my feet, searched and everything in my pockets was tossed on the hood of a nearby cruiser. I was thankful I didn't have the .38 on me.

Jill was panicking, screaming when officers clamped the cuffs down hard on my wrists. She reached out for me but was held back by a half dozen cops. She looked like a troubled baby doll and I found that attractive. Her red hair quickly became a tangled mess. We had talked about getting caught too many times over the last couple of weeks. I also kept her from knowing too much about what Logan and

I were doing all those long months while looking for that pile of embezzled mob money.

But I suspected she might've known all along.

It was all too convenient. She had her sister come over and watch the kids just before we took off for Walmart and then there was the exit door. Walmart had several main entrances. One was located through the garden section. The least amount of people, the least amount of commotion if things went wrong. I should've seen it. She insisted on leaving through that exit. Her moves, the soft touches of fear edged on the tints of her voice. Something didn't ring true in anything she had been doing the last couple of days.

She looked back in anguish. I realized there was more to this than I was being led to believe. The thought tore the pull-strings to my heart.

She had sold me out.

FIVE

It only got worse. I spent a week in lock-up at Torrance County Detention Center. I passed the time pondering the weight of my sins. I was the only inmate in the cell. That suited me fine. I didn't dig into the idea of having to deal with anyone. The Marshals didn't want me talking to anyone either. The prison guards on duty had been instructed not to have any conversation beyond just the usual commands or directions. If they were thinking I was going to crack due to no human contact, they were figuring wrong. But the US Marshals needed me for something. I thought about the angles of the whole mess and how to get my happy-ass out of it. My options were limited.

It had been two weeks since the shootout but it was still big news. The news had made the bold claim I was involved. I wasn't though. I had hidden out with Jill at her house. That was the only angle I had to toy with. After the Dixie boys had finished wrecking my life, they found Logan the same night, kidnapped and took him up to Thomas's house hidden back up in the foothills off Highway 217. But something went wrong, horribly wrong.

I laid my head back against the cold cinder-block wall.

Logan got tied up in the shootout that got five people whacked. I didn't think Logan had it in him to kill a teary-eyed gerbil let alone five bad mother-fuckers from the Dixie Mafia. I nixed that aspect. I focused on the losing team in the shooting.

It didn't hurt my feelings to see Cleeve and Robert Lee were among the dead. God had passed judgment on them for smashing my flat-screen. The troubling part was Thomas had somehow managed to escape. The Feds were looking for him right along with Logan. I crossed Thomas off the mental list. He just managed to cash in on his lucky card.

The surprising element in the mix was Hobart Mills. He was there too and it raised too many questions. Was he connected to the Dixie Mafia? An errand boy? He was just a lube tech at Duggan's and dumb as a box of rocks...or was there something more? The news was claiming he was some sort of big shot within the Dixie Mafia organization. I found that an incredible finding. If that was true, he found something about Logan and I.

Then there was Dwayne the complex manager of Dugan's Truck Stop. I knew he was Dixie Mafia-connected. His side bitch Andrea from book-keeping was also there. Both, just like old Dave Musgrave and Lonnie Blonde, were on the Hell's Express. I wondered how Dwayne held up in the shootout. He hadn't survived but it made me curious about how he went out. Was it like a pussy? Or some kinda Rambo eater super trooper?

There had to be something more. Some critical pieces I hadn't figured in.

The angles. There weren't too many options or so it looked. The top threat to my freedom was the shootout. That was easy enough to eliminate. I wasn't even there.

The fact that the shootout was connected to the money Logan and I had found wasn't any real issue either. Not for me. Logan, on the other hand, was under the pile of shit. I was stuck somewhere in the middle.

The trigger. Amy Hauser. She had to be. She was the main bone of contention in all of it, the root cause. I had told Logan to run away from her but he didn't listen. Amy's old man, Thomas Hauser wasn't too keen on the fact Amy was hooked up with Logan. His pride had been damaged. The money was just an afterthought. His vengeance was destined to be certain and swift. And she was nowhere to be seen.

The opposing team in the shootout.

They were shadowy figures standing within the thick clusters of images and tall forests of darkness. I thought long and hard about who they might be. I couldn't figure out anything about them. Hell, it could be anybody. Mexican cartel groups, another rival mob group, even the Feds. I didn't like the idea of the latter. The US government was too powerful and they could make people disappear quickly.

I leaned back against the wall and swore.

The local news channels were heaping the kindle on the fires every morning and night. Action 13 News Investigates, News 4, Eyewitness News 7, they told all the sordid details in truths and half-truths, predicting fortune-cookie endings. The FBI, ATF, and a whole slew of other Federal alphabet agencies involved only gave vague information. They were too busy in the massive state and national manhunt for Logan and Thomas. I was just a blip in the news. It was all about Logan. That pissed me off for some reason.

The news outlets were giving Logan too much credit. I didn't know where that ass-clown was hiding but he was hiding well. My thoughts drifted back to Amy who was nowhere to be seen. That was troubling. There wasn't a mention of her anywhere.

It all boiled down to the other players, the main dudes who'd done the shooting. I just couldn't put a finger around it. Who were they? How many were there? A few? An army? A vast network?

I gave up thinking about it. It was all too much to think about. The thing I need to focus on was my current predicament. Surely the Marshals, local cops, somebody was interested in me. I didn't have to wait long.

The sounds of boots grew loud and close. The sound came to a stop outside my cell. I could make out the soles of boots. The door buzzed and then popped open. I looked over with tired eyes. A half dozen guards stood there. A sergeant, judging by the tabs on his lapels stepped forward into the cell, holding a clipboard. "Hendricks, step out."

"Shower?"

"Negative. Step out," he repeated.

They weren't offering any explanation. I stepped out where I was instructed to face the wall. I did as I was told while they chained me up. They were taking no chances. After a quick visual examination, the sergeant motioned for me to move out.

We moved out, three guards in front and three behind. We exited the pod and down the hallways. I ignored the look from the inmates piled up against the glass from the surrounding pods. When we reached the booking area, we were met with a trio of US Marshals who looked more annoyed in seeing us flood into the room.

A Marshal Deputy stepped forward, flipped open a manila folder. He looked me up and down a few times. Finally, he asked for the keys, and the sergeant handed them over. Stuffing them in his pocket he motioned for me to follow. We moved outside. The sun was bright, and I held up my shackled hands over my eyes to shield the worst of the glare. I paused, took a deep breath admiring the warmth of the sun, and open-air for the first time in a week.

SIX

I sat in silence across from some scrawny attorney type. He hadn't spoken a single word for the better part of fifteen minutes. Occasionally, he'd look up from his pile of papers, study me over a minute then refocus back on the pile.

The door popped open- two men entered silently. One reminded me of some character out of an eighties TV show *Miami Vice*. He had the suit jacket over jeans and slicked-back hair down to a science. A shoulder rig with a Glock pistol could be seen. He held a cup of coffee in one hand and a manila folder in the other.

The other man was a full head taller. Muscle bulged under his three-piece suit. Nothing special to note other than he had a nice vertical scar over his left eye. His small mustache twitched.

Finally, the scrawny man decided to break the awkward silence.

He picked up a single piece of paper. "You understand you are in some pretty serious trouble."

"I figure so. It's why we're all here, right? Get to the fucking point."

He frowned and settled back to read the papers in his hand. "My name is Corfield, Stan Corfield, assistant US attorney and you might want to watch your language with me, Mr. Hendricks." He settled back into his seat and took a long look at me. "I was sent here from Washington to determine if you are a viable witness in an ongoing investigation. If we…the Federal government, if we decide to and if you cooperate, we will sponsor you."

I looked up to the other men. Their expressions weren't offering any explanation. "Sponsor? What the hell does that mean?"

"It means a lifeline, Mr. Hendricks," Corfield replied. "Or the Witness Protection Program. A new life, a new start within WITSEC."

"And if I don't?" I asked.

He picked up several papers in front of him ignoring my question. "Dixie Mafia connections, your work history, past brushes with law enforcement. I would say you are troublesome. Your only redeeming quality is your military record," he looked up. "A field medic with the US Army with service in Operation Desert Shield and Desert Storm," he paused then added. "You earned the Combat Medical Badge...twice. An impossible feat, I might add."

"Your point?"

"I'm wondering why a man of your capabilities could fall so low."

He was hoping to play on my patriotic loyalty card. I wasn't buying it. "I fulfilled my obligations and paid my dues."

He narrowed his eyes. "Being connected with the Dixie Mafia?"

"I'm not connected," I kept my eyes on those shiny glasses of his. "You understand that first off."

"Will you help or not, Mr. Hendricks?" He demanded in a soft tone.

I took a deep breath. My options were limited. If I helped, maybe I'd be out of the jailhouse. I nodded in agreement. "What do you have?"

He took out a paper and unfolded it. It was a topographical map and he slid it over for me to look at. The map was of Dave Musgrave's ranch. "Point out to me where you found the money please."

I looked it over, noting the ranch house, the barns, and other outbuildings or rather where they might be located. The map was outdated by more than a couple of decades. I leaned back in my chair and shook my head. "It's hard to tell by the map."

"You're refusing to assist in an ongoing federal investigation?"

"Didn't say that. It's hard to tell on the map," I stabbed a finger on the area I felt was close. "This map is outdated first off. There is nothing on here showing where Musgrave had his house or any of the outbuildings. I can kinda guess but that's about it."

"Didn't you use a map?" Corfield asked.

"We did, a much newer one, and we also had it marked with everything including where the buildings were, every junk car, every damned bush."

"May I ask how you found this money?"

"How?"

"I find it strange. You and Logan, a couple of mechanics, found this money when everyone else couldn't. The FBI went out to Musgrave's ranch for several months and didn't find it. But, by some miracle," he paused holding his hands up to the air and looking for God. "Somehow, you and Logan did." He tapped his fingers on the desk.

"So, you guys saying we're smarter than you?"

"It is a coincidence you found its precise location. You knew more than you led on, which leads everyone involved to be believed in having connections within the Dixie Mafia."

"Nothing, believe me, we're not connected," I threw my hands up. "Hell, we're just a couple of diesel mechanics who went out there, using our heads, and we hit the jackpot."

"So you just happened to find the money?"

"We just happened to find the money," I repeated. "Seriously."

"So, are you willing to spend twenty years to life in prison?" He shifted in his seat and leaned forward. "You know a bit more than you are leading on. I advise you to cooperate."

"I'm doing the best I can, I assure you."

Corfield raised a hand. "Perhaps, you don't fully understand the charges you're faced with?" He looked up to Miami Vice man. "Mr. Lane? Would you please?"

Lane stepped forward and opened the folder he had been holding. "Racketeering, conspiracy to commit money laundering charges, conspiracy to selling and delivery of destructive devices…"

"Whoa, whoa, wait up now!" I held up my hands.

Lane continued. "Conspiracy to murder a federal informant…"

"Federal witness? I don't know anything about that! What the hell Federal witness are we talking about?" I protested.

"Of course you do, Amy Hauser?"

"That's a twenty-year charge right there, buddy," quipped Lane.

"Logan's girlfriend?" I shot forward, leaning across the table. "Didn't know about that and that is a fact."

"Oh," Corfield tangled his fingers together, leaned across the table. "But you do and we would like for you to cooperate with us on this matter. This is your last chance, sir."

Amy Hauser. Of all people. I wasn't in on the learning curve but it was evident she was involved and in a big way. I knew she was married to Thomas and had decided to have a serious fling with Logan but beyond that, I knew nothing. "I wouldn't harm her in the least, what the hell you want anyway?"

"Where's Logan and the money?"

"Your guess is as good as mine."

"You are lying," Corfield countered.

"And I'm telling you, I don't know," I added quickly. "I lost my cut a couple of weeks ago when the Dixie boys showed up at my place and ran my ass through the wringer. They found my cut of the money, understand?"

"The shooting?"

"What? You mean over at Thomas's house? I don't know anything about it. I was hiding out with my fiancé Jill. I'm sure she's told you that already."

Corfield shook his head and leaned forward. "She has, as a matter of fact, but you don't care about your friend Logan's safety?"

"Oh? His safety?" They were playing the sympathy card. "Nothing in this deck of cards for me? If any, and I mean any, Dixie Mafia guys come rolling around, imagine what they would do to me?"

"His life is in danger, you understand?"

"I understand. I also understand I'm being detained for questioning. I understand you guys are in a twist and I understand if I tell you things, my life ain't shit."

"It's why we are having this discussion, Hendricks." He tapped his finger on the map laid out between us. "Let us try again. Where was the money located?"

"And what else was in there?" Lane added.

"What else?" I asked.

"Besides the money. Don't play stupid," he looked over to his sidekick. "Brock?"

Brock grunted. "For a few years, we've been looking into some Cartel operating here in the states. Supposedly, they lost a bunch of money and guns. We want all the info you got."

"Dixie Mafia," I looked at Corfield. "Now some Mexican Cartel?"

"San Luis Cartel I might add," Corfield leaned back in his chair, took up a glass of water, and took a sip. "I don't expect you to know or understand everything. But I do expect cooperation."

I figured on an angle. They needed me alive. They needed me to testify, to tell them everything I knew, to help them put the pieces of this puzzle together. It didn't take a rocket scientist long to add two and two. "Guarantees."

"What are those?" Corfield demanded.

"Jill…she comes with me for starters."

Lane sighed and gave a small smile. "She wasn't too kosher with the idea of witness protection."

I leaned back. I shouldn't be surprised. She had the kids- her parents were still alive and her sisters were close emotionally. To leave all of them behind would've been too much. It hurt like hell but I wasn't going to show it. Not to these bastards. "Options?"

Corfield opened up the manila folder in front of him and slid out a single piece of paper. "You sign this and life will get a free pass."

I started to reach over to take a look at the fine print but he pulled it back quickly. "But…you will tell us everything. If not?" He looked up to the ceiling and then slowly back to me. "You can rot in prison for a long time, Mr. Hendricks."

I looked him in the eyes. He was dead serious. Corfield had me by the balls and there wasn't much I could do about it.

"Another thing too," Lane quipped. "Haircut. We want you to look different than the ragged-ass bum you look like."

Brock let off a low giggle, sounding like a couple of boulders colliding.

I started to hate this Lane guy. What the hell other choice was there though?

Corfield smiled. "Let us start from the beginning, shall we?"

SEVEN

"So, I'm reading here from your file you have a drinking problem? Mister..." she thumbed through several pages. "Mister Beck?"

My new name is Ward Beck. The name sounds too close to Lord Dick in my opinion. The Marshals made a goof somewhere in the paperwork though. I was told to expect another name change. Word was another WITSEC candidate was using the same name somewhere else. For the time being, I still had to use the name Beck until my new name came through. I felt sorry for the other guy.

Poor bastard.

"Mr. Beck?"

She was a looker, one of those high-class educated kinds of broads men wanted but never could get close enough to. Young, maybe mid-thirties at the most, high class college material, like the Harvard or Oxford kind. She had soft, long blonde hair and piercing blue eyes, the kind that leaves a mark on your soul and leaves you wanting more. She was all business, which is probably why she made it into the US Marshals.

"No, I like to drink from time to time while watching the game," I said.

She scribbled a few notations on a note-pad on the table. "I have a report here that states you left the facility and went to a bar."

"Is it against the law?"

She lowered her head, peering above her glasses. "Breaking out of a secure safe house under US Marshal control is a problem. We're a little concerned you are not taking your situation seriously. You do realize the…" she paused while thumbing through her notes. "The Marshal's services are also not to be taken lightly either?"

"They should've gone and got me the beer."

She looked up from her notepad. "You understand the Dixie Mafia…is currently looking for you? A contract is out there for your life."

"Beer," I shrugged.

She clicked her pen a few times, studying me. "You refused to leave the bar as ordered."

"The beer was the important thing at the moment."

"It took several Albuquerque Police officers to remove you from the bar, where you then spent a night in Bernalillo County Detention Center."

"You guys at the Marshals should've just gotten me the beer when I asked. Hell, I had the money for it."

"Deputy Marshal Lane had to bail you out."

"Beer, next time, the God damned beer."

"I'm going to venture it's a 'yes' on your problem," she

scribbled a few more notes.

It's a requirement from WITSEC. Everyone goes through counseling sessions. I guess it has to do something with the fact that your life as you've known it is officially over. The old you has died and faded away. Some guys can't handle it. One day they're running at the top of their game, raking in the money, the broads, everything, then the next moment, they're facing life or death and they opt for the US Marshals to step in and help. Their new life identity isn't what it's cracked up to be so they split the scene to visit some old hang-outs, maybe even visit some broads, or a restaurant they loved to go to. It often can be fatal. I'll give the Marshals an ace in never having lost a person within their custody. Those that did die had given up on the WITSEC program and went outside the Marshals protective wing.

In my case, I had asked for a six-pack of brews before the ball game between the Tigers and Angels kicked off but the deputies nixed the request. I took the alternate route. I jimmied the window open in the bathroom, slid out, grabbed a nearby drain pipe, and jumped down into the dark alleyway. I resisted running off right away. I waited several minutes, watching the window above where I had escaped. No one came looking for me. I figured I had about ten minutes to vanish. A bum rustled under a pile of makeshift cardboard, eyeing me as I walked away.

Albuquerque PD found me in the Blue Moon bar. How? I never did know but I was sure some local yahoo was questioned, saw me, and pointed out the last direction he saw me going. I wasn't bothering a soul, just drinking a cold Sam Adams and catching the game on the tube. Things got a little out of hand. I spent a night in lock-up before the Marshals came around.

I could appreciate their concern but I really wanted a beer and catch the game.

Silence filled the room. The only sound was the soft, hushed whisper of the air conditioner flowing from the vents or the occasional scribbling of pen on paper. I turned and looked out the window. Albuquerque is a bustling miniature city. The noontime sun hung high above, the blue skies bright and clear. Jill would be hanging laundry out in the backyard about now. Even though I'd gotten her a drier, she still preferred hanging the laundry outside. The sun always looked so damned good flowing through her hair.

"Mister Beck?"

I refocused. "Here?"

"You seem….lost?"

"Just thinking is all."

"About?"

"About my beer," I said. "Somewhere out there, a beer is missing me."

She leaned back and crossed her shapely legs. "What kind of beer do you like?"

"Are you asking me out for a nightcap?"

She ignored the remark. "I'm making it a point to make sure we never go through this again. I'm also making sure you have your beer. Maybe you should try and look for another brand of beer, wean off your regular brand and reduce your intake."

I continued with my own thought. "Usually, it's the guy who asks the woman out for a drink. I've never had a woman hit on me before." I looked up at her with mock surprise.

"You think this is a joke?"

"No," I answered. "I'm confused if you're asking me out or not. I'm getting a lot of mixed signals."

"Twenty-years, Mister Beck," she looked at me over the glasses again. "That's what you're facing, and if I recall correctly, you agreed to our terms of protection a couple of weeks ago, and already, you're proving to be troublesome."

"Get me the beer next time."

She picked up the pen and scribbled more notations. "I'm going to recommend more counseling sessions," she looked up. "I think you could benefit from it if you apply yourself."

"Will you be given the sessions?"

She fell silent shaking her head. Her face flushed with a tinge of red. I couldn't tell if she was blushing or if it was a rise in anger.

"Maybe a few brews and we'll see what happens?" I pressed.

"I'm spoken for," she answered but it was a cold response.

"Lucky guy."

She picked up the tablet, stood up, and opened the file. She handed me a paper. "It says you're going to Wyoming, Mr. Beck. I hear it gets cold and windy up there. Maybe you should pack some cold-weather gear," she shut the manila folder. "I'll pass your file off to the field counselor there and maybe he can help you where I cannot."

"So, no date?" I looked at the paper. "No phone number?"

She ignored the question, walked out of the room, a cold wisp of air trailed behind her.

Brock was waiting outside. She stopped. She spoke to him, anger in her tone. When she left Brock stepped in and motioned for me to follow. He held the door open. "You got balls," he grumbled while shaking his head.

"She looked too good to pass up," I said

He hit the elevator button and the doors slid open. "She's a lesbian."

We stepped into the elevator. "Really?" I whispered.

He nodded, pressed the first-floor button. "Her 'spouse' would've broken you in two if she'd heard you saying those things."

"Sounds like a good time," I countered.

EIGHT

I spent several months at a Federal safe house in Denver. I went through the do and do-not of the WITSEC program. One of the things I managed to get was beer from time to time when I requested it. That was the only thing positive to come from those damned counseling sessions. I never saw the blonde bombshell again or any other woman counselor. She was replaced by some guy who took a serious interest in my plight. He kinda reminded me of an older version of Ward Cleaver from the old TV show *Leave it to Beaver* but a bit smaller in stature. He seriously tried to help but somethings won't change.

My new identity is Alan Moore. Not too bad a name and simple to remember. Basic info is I was widowed after a five-year marriage, no kids, born in some small shit-kicker town out in

Nebraska, dropped out of high school and got a GED. Simple backdrop. But there were a few mistakes. I didn't get a commercial driver's license and nothing on a military background. In other words, no prior military experience which, boils down to no VA benefits or GI Bill access.

The last items pissed me off to no end. Despite everything I had done for the greater cause for America and the Army, the Marshals had tossed my service record. I had served in Desert Shield and Desert Storm, and the Marshals had disregarded my request about military benefits. I believed it was Lane and Corfield's way of sticking it up my ass for running off in Albuquerque.

I was set to restart life on the wind-swept plains of Wyoming in a town called Gillette. I had given up most of all my information about the money and how we found it to the Feds. We made a single outing to Musgrave's ranch followed by an army of FBI agents and State Police. We took the long stroll up through the property where the conex storage container was buried. I pointed out the single, worn ancient telegraph pole, and the conex was unearthed. I heard it took a couple of days to remove the massive amount of guns stored down there. In exchange, once the guns were recovered, I was given a new identity and thrown out to fend for myself.

Of course, the Feds reserved the right to come knocking on my door anytime to ask for more information, to clarify current information, or just to bust my balls.

The worst was pending court dates. I was told the possible itinerary of any court appearance sometime in the future. Lane made sure I was uncomfortable. There was something about the asshole I didn't like. Besides the holier-than-though attitude, the Miami Vice attire, there was a streak of sadistic sarcasm he and his boyfriend Brock enjoyed. There wasn't a damn thing I could do about it either and they knew it.

I was given a few months to get back up on my feet, a small cash allowance per month, and a rental house just off the main drag in Gillette. Oilfield companies and workers moved pipes and material all through the town. I was left hanging, unable to acquire decent employment. I had no commercial driver's license and that ruled me out of driving truck. Any diesel mechanic certifications I had held in my old life got tossed to the wind. Any manager with any kind of sense would have a good chuckle reading over the resume the Marshals had drafted up.

I had a basic background in mechanics and had to start over on the ground floor in my career...again. Even though I had twenty years' experience, nothing could be verified. I was forced to take a job as a lube tech working at some small shop that paid jack-shit squat.

I surmised Lane had a hand in it. The background checks always came back spotty, or there was something the oilfield recruiters found wrong or missing. Lane and his crew were supposed to cover up these holes, but they hadn't. So the bigger money jobs were passing me up.

I cursed day and night of this wretched new life I found myself in. I made a vow to reclaim my old life. I vowed vengeance.

NINE

I was downing a glass of Jack and Coke at the local bar when I first heard the news about Logan getting captured up in Minnesota. It was November. The cold winds and snows of winter had settled across the rolling hills. Oil field traffic remained constant. I was still feeling the sting of losing out on jobs as a certified diesel mechanic. A few shots into tomorrow's hangover only helped marginally in taking the edge off.

I wasn't a bit happy about my new home here in Gillette. Anyone who's ever been there knows it's full of fucking rolling hills, the wind blows, the broads chew tobacco, and the men suck meth to keep going in the oilfields. With Jill not in the picture anymore, I was going bat-shit bonkers and took the alcohol closer to heart.

A couple of other guys at the bar laughed at the news feed of

Logan running through some truck stop parking lot. They made comical comments when Logan got tackled and slammed to the snow-packed asphalt.

It wasn't funny.

It's easy to make fun of something you don't understand. Logan had been on the run for almost six months. Looking over the two idiots laughing at the bar, I doubted they could survive a day running from the Dixie Mafia or the Feds. Even though Logan was a pussy-whipped idiot, he made a hell of an effort keeping low and running for as long as he did.

Hell, I made it only two weeks before the Feds came around, and I considered myself a bit street-savvy. I had wondered where he was at and knew it was just a matter of time before the Feds or the Dixie boys from Mississippi finally caught up with him. Fear is a great motivator that pushes men to greater action.

One of the men laughing at the television leaned over and commented. "You looking like you're sad he was caught," he chugged a beer. "Hell, that guy had a helluva bounty on him. Wish I'd found him."

"But you didn't, which means you ain't smart."

He lowered the beer mug. "Huh?"

"See? You ain't a bright one."

The barstool slid back and the bear rose. He stood a half-head taller and leered through a toothless grin. "You were implying something?"

I slammed the shot glass down on the bar. The golden elixir splashed over my hand and the counter. The nearby bar patrons fell silent. On the television, Logan was being escorted back to a police cruiser and disappeared into the back seat. "You heard me, dumb-shit."

He looked back to his partner who stood up.

"What? You gotta get permission from your wife before you do anything besides stand there with your dick in your hand?"

Of course, that's when the fight started. There's nothing like working out your aggression with your hands.

When the cops got there, the three of us sat perched on our bar stools, nursing wounds, and tumblers of booze. Even though we worked out our issues and told the bar owners we'd pay damages, they were just pricks about it. These days, it seems no one can have a little fun and work out a bit of aggression anymore.

The cops weren't too sure who I was since my background was sketchy on the background check. They thought I was hiding information on who I was. I stuck to everything the WITSEC people had taught me from the beginning: lie.

The cops decided to haul me in.

Once we were downtown, they proceeded to give me the riot act in telling them who I was. I stuck to the lie just as I was told to. They weren't satisfied and I wasn't going to tell them jack-shit. The fingerprints were coming back with nothing. That raised a few more red flags. After an hour, they gave up and locked me away in a cell and life moved on.

By morning though, I was itching for a brew. The jailer, Officer McIntire, looked way too young to be taken seriously as a cop. He looked every bit of fifteen years old even though he was probably pushing thirty. No one took him seriously which was probably one reason why he was shafted into inmate duty. He came around to pick up the empty trays from morning breakfast. The cells were holding the usual town drunks and hell-raisers who couldn't post bail or refused to.

I handed my tray through the slot. "When the fuck am I getting out of here?"

McIntire took my tray and gave a cold response. "When you decide to tell us who you are, cupcake."

I broke the line and went for broke. "Okay…you got me." I held my hands up. A big shit-eating grin spread on my face.

He continued holding the tray. "Got you?"

"Yeah, look, my real name is James Albert Hendricks. I'm hiding from some mob group known as the Dixie Mafia. You ever heard of them?"

He shook his head.

"A buddy and I got tangled up in some shit down in New Mexico. I'm in the Witness Protection Program."

He tossed the tray on the cart and rolled his eyes. "Ha-ha, funny man."

"No, seriously. You heard about those five dead mob dudes and the state cops all tangled up in drugs and gun dealing down in New Mexico?" I pointed a thumb at my chest. "Right here, *boyo*."

"Bullshit, they got the guy," referring to Logan. "You're just a guy who's hiding from the law. Where did you come from? What are you hiding?"

"How about you do your job and really look it up." I pressed my face against the bars. "You see, me and my buddy Logan, we found a half-million in cash…"

He rolled his eyes in disbelief. "Cash, huh? And this Logan is your buddy?"

"Yeah, but we knew it belonged to the Dixie Mafia. They came looking for their money. A few…well, more than a few, people got killed."

"You?" He snorted and started to move off.

"And the best part? Once the Mafia catches wind I'm in here? They're going to come in this town and start killing everyone in their way to get to me. I got a hit out on me now."

He stayed quiet- his frown twitched.

I pressed in further, dropping my voice to a whisper. "Are you and the Barney Fife gang ready for what's coming? How about your families? This town will get fucking wiped off the face of the earth."

"Bullshit."

"Try it."

We locked eyes momentarily before he shoved the cart forward.

McIntire looked into it. The next day, a couple of Marshals Deputies and Lane showed up. The deputy sheriff opened the cell door. Lane stood there with his hands in his pockets. His frown told everyone he was agitated. He motioned for me to get out of the cell.

"Boy am I…"

He cut me off with a wave of his hand. "Not now."

I sighed and stepped out into the hall. Lane nodded and I was told to hold out my hands. I was surprised when the handcuffs ratcheted around my wrists. I gave a puzzled look to Lane. He wasn't smiling.

After several minutes in booking, signing off on the paperwork, I was a free man. But only for a little bit. Now I had to face the wrath of Lane. He was visibly pissed as he signed off on the papers, stabbing hard with each pen stroke.

We walked out of the police station without a word, just the sounds of our feet clobbering the concrete. Two Ford Explorers sat alongside the curb. Several other agents milled around them. Lane grabbed hold of the door handle and opened the back door for me. During the whole episode, I was still in handcuffs.

"Would you mind?" I held out my shackled hands.

"Get in," came Lane's curt response.

I shook my head, sighed, and slid into the back seat. Lane slammed the door shut. He took a moment to compose himself before opening the passenger door and seating himself in front. Another Marshals deputy I didn't know slid in behind the wheel and fired off the engine but didn't move. The cab was silent.

"How long am I going to be handcuffed," I started.

"When I see fit to remove said handcuffs," Lane answered.

"C'mon, this isn't necessary is it?"

"I wish you were quiet and as cooperative as your buddy."

I knew he was referring to Logan. "I heard he got caught. How's he doing these days?"

Lane took off his sunglasses and turned to face me. He could see it was a bait question. "He's quiet and cooperative maybe take some notes on the subject."

"Well, shit, how about giving something to climb up on?"

He looked puzzled.

"How about getting me a CDL? Or maybe some damn engine certifications? I had a lot of paper backing me up in getting some decent mechanics jobs." I looked out the window again. An old man was walking his dog nearby. It reminded me time is a fleeting thing. "Right now, I'm a damn lube tech making barely above minimum. No manager is taking me seriously on anything."

"You were supposed to get your commercial driver's license. The rest is up to you to get…," he turned away, facing the windshield. "We can't just pull papers out of our butts without a solid background."

"Oh, cry me a fucking river, Lane! You can talk to someone in your department! How in the hell am I supposed to make this work if I'm living on starvation wages? At least give me something a bit more viable than being a fucking lube tech!"

"I have. It was clear about the CDL," he exhaled. A silence fell in the car before he turned his head, his eyes looking back. "This is not up for debate, Hendricks. You're turning into an expense, not an asset. Knock off your bullshit. I am not going to bail you out of jail again."

A few weeks later, I found myself down in bum-fuck Texas and received additional counseling sessions.

TEN

My new name is George Olsen. Jesus, what a boring name. I mean, what woman in her right mind would bed down with a guy named George? But, I guess that was the intent of name changes. You are supposed to be low-key. The name was supposed to suck. I was sure someone up in WITSEC thought the shit was funny.

I boarded a puddle jumper in Dallas with several other US Marshals deputies at four am. We landed in Fort Stockton right around eight. During the trip, I took a few pulls from a bottle of Crown Royal samplers I had managed to secret away in my bags. Brock watched me with unconcern as I downed a few samplers. I caught his gaze and muttered a curse. I leaned back to him. "I get nervous before a flight," I said.

"Funny," he remarked. "I don't recall you drinking any on the previous ones we've been on."

"I'm a bit crafty sometimes," I replied with narrowed eyes.

He shook his head, grunted before flipping up his newspaper, cutting off any further conversation.

When we hit the tarmac in Fort Stockton, Lane was waiting beside a black Ford Explorer with his hands in his pockets. The tails to his suit jacket fluttered in the wind, revealing a Glock .40 hanging off his hip.

The Marshals shuttled me to some oil field town named Orla. The surprising thing about it was I was located a mere fifty miles or so from the New Mexico border. With everything that had happened there, I figured they would've kept me as far away from the Land of Enchantment as much as possible.

I hired on as a field mechanic with a crude oil hauling outfit just outside Monahans, Texas. I guess Lane had some sympathy and produced a CDL license and a few minor documents related to my diesel mechanic trade. It wasn't much, but it was a start. My background stated I had close to eighteen years' experience in the trucking industry. Most of the trucking companies listed or mentioned on my new resume were out of business or absorbed by larger trucking outfits. Paperwork gets easily lost in the shuffle when those kinds of events happen in the industry.

WITSEC should've done that from square one, I thought, but Lane was an ass about it for some reason. We said nary a word as we drove up Highway 285. The desolate desert of brown colors washed up to the distant horizon of deep blue skies. Oil rigs were busy drilling for the black gold that lay some two to three miles deep under the desert floor. Semis hauling crude oil, wastewater, or fracking sand rolled up and down the highway, feeding the oilfields with as many supplies as it could handle.

I had made the resolve to forget about Jill. It was a difficult choice, but life had to move on. I couldn't stand still in time and hope she would come along with me. I was where I was in life. Deep down, and in my dreams, I thought about her too much. Inside my heart, I had resolved to put her memory on hold. There would be no changing it for now.

We rolled up into a large dirt lot packed with derelict Peterbilts on the outer fringes of a dirt town named Orla. Lane helped to get a job lined up. He had a few connections in these parts. The company he chose was an oil hauler outfit. They ran a fleet of Peterbilts from varying years and models. Once we stopped at the yard, I stepped out of the back of the Explorer and stretched. At first glance, the rag-tag group of trucks looked like they had done a couple of tours in Iraq. Hoods sat crooked, tires were flat, and the broken windshields told me I had my work cut out for me.

"Don't look so disappointed, Hendricks."

"It's George," I corrected him.

Brock looked at me. A small smile playing across his face.

"Just checking to see if you're catching on," Lane handed me up a business card. "We got some guys staying around here to help keep an eye on things. If you run into problems, you know what to do."

I took the card. The standard protocol was to call in and give a code. You were then instructed to call back on another line. This second line was supposed to be secure. From that point on, you explained what happened or expressed your concerns. I tucked the card away in my shirt pocket. "What now?"

Lane smiled and pointed to the office. "You go in there and the boss will set you up. I heard they got a fairly large man camp on the edge of town."

I frowned. The idea of staying in a man camp wasn't exactly what I wanted, but there was no other real viable option.

He saw the frown. His smile widened. "Relax, maybe you'll find someone to keep you warm on those long, lonely nights."

Brock gave a rumbling laugh under his breath.

Ignoring the comment, I took up my old duffle bag and other handbags. These held the remnants of my tattered life. Nothing much, just clothes, paperwork, and a few personal mementos. Nothing bulky. "Fuck you, Lane."

He gave off a low laugh.

The Texas heat washed over me. It was a welcomed relief from the air-conditioned chill with my current company inside the Explorer.

"Remember, stay out of trouble," Lane said. "You might end up in prison the next time."

"Not me," I answered.

"We'll see," Lane pushed his sunglasses up the bridge of his nose. "Chow, baby."

Before I could say anything, he took off in a cloud of dust and hit the pavement back south on 285. I muttered a curse. If I could ever catch that son of a bitch in a dark alley, I'd light him up enough to fear the flames of Hell.

ELEVEN

Hyperion Oil Field Service was just another small-time operator employing some one hundred and fifty drivers bouncing around the Permian Basin. Their main gig was hauling crude oil. The main base of operations was in the town of Monahans situated some eighty miles away. The oil prediction was a boom was building up. Every company in the area was bracing for it.

Oil field traffic was steady but light unless it was early morning or afternoon, then it was bumper to bumper. The end-of-year projection from the big boys of the field was something around 1.6 million barrels of raw crude to be pumped from deep within the earth's crust. It was shaping up that I was being dealt a fair hand on the money end. I was at the tip of the spear on making bank.

I hired on as a field mechanic and was issued a one-ton

Chevrolet service truck. It had a crane, welder, and torch set, but no other tools. The usual setup complementing any service truck running the field. I hit the pawn shops in Kermit and Fort Stockton and managed to scrounge up a fair amount of tools. I knew I would need as many tools in the arsenal for the battles that lay ahead. I talked Lane into giving me some cash. He grilled my ass about it demanding receipts for every little thing I purchased. I guess he was making sure I wasn't out drinking and throwing money around on whores. Fair enough.

Hyperion had a shop with about four mechanics working in Monahans. The mechanics lacked everything from tools to knowledge, the latter being the critical missing element. They had hired on a few guys who professed to be the gods of the mechanic world. It showed.

If I could ever catch the recruiter for Hyperion, I was going to kick him in the balls for hanging out at Jiffy Lube and trying to recruit the lube techs. These guys were dyed in the wool idiots. Everything they touched had a reversed Medusa effect. It usually turned to shit. My call-outs in the dead of night increased due to the level of stupidity committed by the shop mechanics. Management didn't seem to give two-shits about the problems their 'master' mechanics were creating either.

I was being dealt a bad hand in the barrage of battle damage on the trucks and trailers. Front springs and spring hangers shattered, differential gears shattered, clutch burned, frames and mounts cracked, and motors shelled from lack of maintenance. The mechanics didn't bother to change oil let alone grease anything. They pencil-whipped the paperwork and sent it. That made the job much more difficult. The dumb shits couldn't grasp the fact a little grease and fresh oil went a long way.

I cursed the calls knowing full well the yard mechanics didn't take any call-outs during the night time. I was solo in that arena. The phone calls never stopped, but then again, neither did the money. My bank account swelled. I was glad for the one silver lining swirling around in the chaos. I felt I'd earned every damned penny of it regardless of what management thought.

When I wasn't working out in the field, I was busting my ass back at the yard, cobbling and rebuilding trucks and tankers, hoping to God on High the units would survive the night without a mishap. Sometimes, it was a simple repair, maybe a light, a fuse, or relay, but then there were those calls I was asked to do the impossible. Axles on trailers snapped off, trucks collapsed when a front spring broke, or engine fans ate the radiators when a mount broke. Those jobs made me want to go postal on the shop guys and management. But I held it in. I didn't need any flak from the Marshals or additional counseling sessions.

Working in the oil fields is an unusual phenomenon. As a mechanic or truck driver, the experiences differ vastly from the world of trucking. The over-the-road driver steers a well-maintained truck on smooth asphalt highways to all corners of America from coast to coast. They complain about bad seats, front end vibrations, and busted wiper blades. They have their asses wiped with lavish compliments about what Hero-of-the-Highways they are.

The oil field driver? He's lucky if he sees any asphalt. He's praying his hemorrhoids get a slim chance to drive on some smooth blacktop at least sometime during his route. But the liquid Gold is buried deep in the desolate interiors of Texas and New Mexico. The chances of asphalt roads are next to none. The truck drivers operate battered machines that look like something out of a cheap B-grade apocalypse film. Loaded down with raw crude, they maneuver across a system of crudely cut dirt roads, racing to an offload center like it's a Baja 500 race.

This was why there was such a high turnover rate.

On my first day at orientation, there was something like fifteen drivers present. By the end of the month, all of these same drivers were gone. Some quit the first day once they saw the truck they were going to driving. Others quietly ran away in the middle of the night. Hauling crude oil wasn't for everyone.

After a time, I didn't even want to know anyone's name. There were those drivers who had been around for some time. I knew their names, even broke bread, and drank beer with some of them. But the others? They became forgotten footnotes in the vaults of memory. The 'quitting virus' wasn't limited to drivers. Soon, it spread over to the mechanics. It started with one and then, like an avalanche, followed by three others. Once the dust settled, there was only a mechanic named Ricardo left standing. He might've not known much but he made one hell of an effort in trying. We became close friends, not as close as many but we tolerated one another. I knuckled down a notch, often staying until the early hours fixing trucks or tankers at the yard or pulling rigs out of sand traps.

There were times I forgot who I was supposed to be. I knew I was supposed to be George Olsen but the James Hendricks was always there, lurking in the shadows of memory. I felt like the same guy but with a make-believe name and life, forced to live in a make-believe world. I slipped a few times in mentioning my old name. I did a few times, but the person didn't appear a bit concerned when I let it slip.

During the lulls of the hustle of the oilfields, I was in a trance from sleep deprivation. I sat watching the sunrise or fall below the horizons, the moon following the same vicious cycle. The landscape was both hostile and unforgiving. The beauty of nature at work made me take a moment and appreciate it all. It made me temporarily forget about Logan, Duggan's Truck Stop, the Dixie Mafia, the US Marshals, and Jill.

The keyword was almost.

TWELVE

The headlights on the Chevy jolted, dipped, and rose through the inky darkness only to drop down to face the silty sands of the Texas desert. The speakers were belting out Soil's song *Halo*. Nothing like a bit of hard rock while dealing with the crap road. The road was a rough cut goat-trail across the Texas plains known as CR 29. Besides the soft silt flowing over the path, there were patches of hardcore washboard that shook loose the stinging dirt from a man's pores. The insatiable quest for black gold reached deep into the distant interiors of unexplored deserts stretching for miles.

The Bakken Basin was the top dog in oil production. The Permian Basin was small potatoes compared to the millions of barrels pumped out in North Dakota, but we were catching up. Word around the campfire was the Permian was slated for a boom. I had heard this rumor from the beginning. I just hoped, in some ways, the rumor wasn't true. There was no way our small operator fleet could survive a boom. We were too ragged an operation. Most of the big oil companies were shying away from using our services as it was. We made all kinds of promises to deliver, but we didn't have the equipment to sustain.

That was troubling. If this company was nosed-diving, where would I go? I was sure I could find something. There were other outfits, other competitors, but would they hire me if the oil market bottomed out?

I rolled to a stop, flipped on the cab interior light, and looked down at the crumpled piece of paper in my hand. On the paper were rough, hand-drawn sketches of most of the well sites in the area. Everyone working in the oilfields knows these kinds of maps. They mean 'we-don't-really-know-where-the-fuck-the- sites-are' kind of maps. They looked like they'd been hand-scrawled with a black marker by some kid in first grade.

I looked up through the windshield, noting the distant well site known as '*Deep Star*'. The rig lights burned bright much like a beacon of hope throughout the dark lands. I tried to work my ass back out of the bush and onto anything familiar, preferably with an asphalt road. I wasn't having too much luck.

Having enough of trying to route my ass back out of the area, I took to another idea: wait for daybreak where the darkness faded enough to light the landscape, and also, where the oil field traffic was concentrated by the steady stream of headlights. My phone said the timeline was an hour off and besides, I was flipping tired. I leaned back in the seat. Sleep was easy out in the field. Sometimes, that invites trouble.

From the whispery tendrils of sleep-induced fog, the Iraqi, a familiar acquaintance from Desert Storm dreamland, materialized, but the thick soup obscured his features. The only way I could tell it was him was from the bloody white sheet he clutched over his belly. He shuffled forward, slow and deliberate, moaning in agony, dragging intestines behind him. There was a sound of buzzing somewhere. It grew louder and louder.

I gasped and awoke with a start, choking, jumping in the seat wondering where I was before recognizing the familiar panels and interiors of the service truck.

My phone buzzed, lighting up the interior of the cab. I moaned and reached over and flipped it open. "This George," I croaked.

The familiar voice rang a distant bell. "It's good you remember your name."

"What do you want, Lane?" I had high hopes of never hearing from him again, but here we were.

"It's showtime," he answered.

"Showtime? What the fuck you mean?" I clamped my eyes shut, squeezing the bridge of my nose with dirt-encrusted fingers trying to push back the residual memory of the dead Iraqi. He was slowly fading, retreating into the depths of unwanted memories.

"It's time for you to live up to your part of the bargain."

I sat up in the seat, moaned softly. I understood then what he meant. "When?"

"We'll be there tomorrow…morning, early."

"This is bad timing, you know that?"

"I'm sure your boss will understand. I talked to him already, so pack a bag."

THIRTEEN

We took the red-eye express in the early dawn hours of the dying night. The plane arched across the dark skies to Denver. It was the only time I had a break from working the grind of the oilfields. I was feeling a sense of dread at what the outside world had become. When the Marshals came around, I had ten minutes to clean up before we pushed on to Odessa to catch a puddle-jumper to Dallas. Once in Dallas, we waited around for a small bit before jumping a leer jet to Denver.

I had too much time waiting and too many brews before the plane took off from Odessa. Being away from civilization for the last six months had made me thirsty. I had a few more on the flight until Lane and Brock called nix on my seventh round of Wild Turkey after I started sexually harassing the blonde flight attendant.

When the wheels hit the tarmac, we moved quickly and silently out of the plane. A trio of Ford Explorers waited for us. We loaded up and took off across the airport tarmac and out into the wilds of Denver. We got to the federal building and had a few hours to kill. It gave me time to sober up a bit and, of course, instructed on my duties in testimony.

On the stand, I gave the truth, the whole truth, and nothing but the truth. I got grilled by the defense for the better part of a couple of hours. All the legal mumbo-jumbo gave me a headache. I believe I repeated the story twenty times over before everyone got the point.

I waited outside the courtroom, fumbling for a cigarette. Brock was reading a Cosmopolitan magazine. Heidi Klum starred back with longing eyes and a short skirt.

"You mind?" I held up a cigarette.

"No smoking," he didn't see the need to lower the magazine to answer.

I tilted my head. I didn't believe him. "C'mon...I just saw a judge and lawyer come back in from there," I pointed to a door that led outside. "You can't tell me no one around here smokes."

He sighed, lowered the magazine, looked around then stood up. "Alright, two minutes, got it?"

"Understood."

I popped the door open and stepped out onto the open decked area when I saw her. My heart jumped. I shot a look back inside the main hall. Brock had settled back into reading his magazine and Lane was nowhere to be seen. I was sure they wouldn't approve of having two material witnesses talking to each other. Especially if they were connected to the same case.

She looked like some kind of angel that had fallen from the skies of bright blue. She looked back once and turned away while smoking a cigarette. I couldn't ever recall her smoking except for maybe a few times. The anxiety of having to go on trial as a material witness must've been too much.

I remembered when she came to Duggan's Truck Stop. I knew she was going to be a problem. She was married to Thomas Hauser, a well-known Dixie Mafia enforcer. I warned Logan to avoid her. But he didn't. Their affair carried over for months. At least until that night when the devil came calling to claim his rewards. The night that got all of us tossed into WITSEC. I got an ass-beating from the Devil's Dog Pound. Then, after my hasty escape, they went to Logan's place and about killed him.

Amy had been there but had gotten away leaving Logan to his fate. She'd been working for the FBI as an informant. I was hearing she called the Feds in for help. I wasn't sure about the details, but she had been gathering evidence right out from under everyone's noses and passing the information to the Feds for the better part of a year. Not only had she managed to gather the information from the Duggan's Truck Stops computer database, but she also had intimate knowledge of the inner workings of the Dixie Mafia. I knew she was involved in a few things. Word was Thomas pimped her out from time to time to only the elite in society but for financial gains or other things Mob related. I also knew she had a drug problem, at least back then, but now she looked to be in relatively good health.

I wondered how God could pack so much sin in such a small package.

"Amy…" I whispered just loud enough for her to respond.

She looked over, her eyes studying me through those large dark-shaded sunglasses you could barely see her eyes. "I'm afraid you have me confused with someone else."

I could see why Logan became transfixed on her. That syrupy southern tone could lull a man into doing almost any crime. "I get that a lot these days," I answered while firing up a smoke.

"And you are?" She tilted her head and smiled.

I shook my head, gave a half-smile, and played along. "Olsen…George Olsen."

"Ava…Ava Williams," she held out her hand and we shook.

"You work around here? Or you here for business?" I was casting out the fishing line for information, hoping for a bite.

"I think both you and I know, Mister Olsen, anyone here on hallowed Federal grounds would mean it's for business purposes, wouldn't you think?"

I eyed the ring on her finger. "I take it there is a Mister Williams?"

She smiled. "Why, you are observant."

I looked back over the gauzy gloom hanging over the city. "And how is he doing?"

She looked away, studying the city. "He is fine, much better now considering what he's gone through." She changed the subject. "And is there a Miss's Olsen?"

I looked over at her then back over the city. "No."

She was quiet a moment before answering. "I am sorry to hear that, truly, I am."

"Nothing to be sorry about. It happens."

"It's funny how we sometimes don't get what we all want in life, isn't it?"

I studied the distant mountain ranges. I couldn't think of a response.

"You know, there will be someone else that will be more than happy to fill that void in your life," she was sincere in the statement. "In time."

"Time isn't much."

"There will be."

"What are you guys doing now?" I asked, still prodding for

information.

She grinned slightly. "We live a quiet life, Mr. Olsen. I doubt the Marshals would appreciate you knowing too much information on our whereabouts these days."

I looked away, sighed in defeat. "I had to try."

"It was a valiant effort."

The door squeaked open behind us. A few men stepped out into the courtyard and walked up to us. The taller of the three held up a paper. "Ava? Ava Williams?"

She turned and gave a smile. "Yes?"

The agent gave a nod. "It's time."

"She pulled up the sleeve on her shirt, exposing a small, gold watch. "Already?" She then looked up at me. "It's been a nice visit, Mr. Olsen."

I flipped the butt away, jamming my hands in my pockets. "I'll see you guys around sometime."

She smiled, the kind of smile that can slice a soul in two, slid the sunglasses down the bridge of her nose, and her eyes narrowed to slits. "I don't think we will, Mister Olsen, but you do take care." She walked away just ahead of the trio of men. The door slammed behind them. I looked back over the gloom and smog.

I realized I was truly on my own.

FOURTEEN

The Marshals dumped me off without so much as a thank you or kiss my ass. I asked them to pull over at the local dollar store where they sold the only brews in town. When I came back outside, they were nowhere to be seen. I looked around and the bastards had driven off. It would've been pointless calling them back. They would've just laughed and kept going. I began the short trek back to the man-camp by cutting across a weed-choked field. The camp lay just on the other side anyway. Besides, I needed the exercise and the fresh air to purge the Denver smog out of my lungs.

Taking the rest of the day off to regroup was what I needed. I wasn't going to bother calling the boss man until noon tomorrow. It was time to knock back a few brews and maybe catch a flick or two. Once I was back in my camper, I turned on the TV and began cooking up some grub. A sharp rap at the door turned my attention away from the sports segment of the news. Opening the door revealed a smiling grill of bright teeth. Clutched in one hand, Manny Alejo, a driver for Hyperion, held a camouflaged patterned backpack. He held a couple of bottles of tequila in the other.

I took hold of the pack. "Damn, you got it."

"I always get what you need, no?" He replied.

"You do, Manny. I thank you." Some months ago, I had asked for a special request. Manny always made a monthly run to Mexico. If he ever ran across an M9 medic kit, I would pay a pretty penny for it. You could get one here in the States but it was a watered-down civilian version. I wanted the real deal. He smiled and I thought he had forgotten, but he produced what I needed. I turned away and set the backpack down on the table and began unzipping the pockets and examined the contents.

Manny trailed in behind and set the bottle of tequila down on the counter. He began rummaging through the cabinets for a couple of glasses. "Why you need this?" He queried.

"Never know what you're going to run into out here," I replied. "We've both seen plenty of accidents."

He found a couple of glasses, paused, and looked at the bag. "You a doctor?"

I smiled. "No, I was a..." I paused, remembering what the Marshals program had taught me. It still chapped my ass I couldn't say anything about my military experience. "I studied medicine for a time in college." I unzipped the bag, folding it open. "It was a long time ago."

He downed a shot of tequila. "It was a problem getting back across the border with this."

I held up a package of tubes marked morphine sulfate injection, ten milligrams. The plastic tubes were unused and sealed. The packaging stated they were manufactured in Maryland, USA. "I would imagine so. I would ask how you got the pack, but I think it's safe to say I'd rather not know."

He smiled while pouring shots into the two glasses. "In Mexico, you find everything."

Besides the morphine injections, there were a few vials of Novocain, Narcan, Phenergan, Epi-pens along with the more common Pepto-Bismol and single-use acetaminophen pill packs. I also found a single vial of Fentanyl. Just a few milligrams could kill anyone if administered wrong. This potent drug appealed to some druggies for some reason. The bag also had a wide array of bandages, wraps, cravats, iodine swabs. For the money I gave out, I got a pretty damned good return on my investment.

Manny nudged an arm, holding a shot glass of tequila. "I bought plenty of this also. It is the best medicine."

I took the glass and couldn't agree more. I downed half a glass and let the clear liquor settle in the pit of my stomach. I smiled. "Damn good," I gasped. "You went to a better brand?"

He shook his head. "No, they were out of my brand. This only brand I could get."

After refilling my glass, we got down to the basics of men talk, mostly about the job. Manny filled me with the details about the rumors swirling around about the company. It was going to either fold up or get bought out. The supervisors had a meeting of the minds with the drivers while I had been away. Things were tight financially, but they were expecting a turn-around in the next upcoming year.

I had my doubts.

On the fifth shot, Manny looked around. "I notice you have no pictures of a family...or a woman," he leaned back on the couch. "No woman?"

I poured myself my sixth shot. "No, no woman,"

He grunted with a grin. "It is no good for a man to be alone."

I smiled. "Says the man who has a woman in about every town in the southwest. You are hogging them all."

"And I have pictures of all of them. You don't? Or maybe there is one special to you?"

I looked down at the bottom of my glass. Silently, I poured another round. "There was one."

He grunted but didn't say anything, waiting for me to continue.

Taking a sip, I talked softly. "One helluva red-head up in New Mexico."

"Redheads..." Manny smiled.

"A true redhead, not the dyed kind trying to pass for one."

"New Mexico, you say she is there?"

"Was," I swallowed half a shot. I looked up to Manny, smiled, and leaned back to get my wallet out. I was breaking the Marshals protocol, but I didn't give a damn at the moment. I dug around a few moments before pulling out a battered photo. The photo was of Jill and me standing in front of my old camper, each holding a beer bottle. My free hand wrapped around her waist.

He took it and gasped in surprise. "What is this woman's name?"

"Jill," I said.

"Monroe?" He questioned.

Shocked, I leaned forward. "How in the hell would you know that?"

He handed the photo back and smiled. "You spoke of her just a few weeks ago. Remember? At the far end of the camp with Rubin, Ricardo, and the other drivers?"

"I did?" I asked.

"You were drunk, *amigo*," he smiled.

A few weeks back, I did tie one on but I didn't recall how bad.

"Did I say anything else?"

He shook his head, downing a shot. "Something about really missing her." He looked up. "You should go see her. Get this thing out of your system."

I planted my face in my palms. "Nothing else?"

He shook his head. "Naw, *nada*, nothing."

I took up the bottle. "You sure?" That was all I needed was the Marshals to show up and toss my life back up in the air.

"What are you worried about? You said nothing but good things about this woman. It almost made me miss mine."

I pulled the bottle close. "Wait, are you married?"

"No, but if I was I would have missed her. You must go see this woman before many men take an interest in her."

I frowned. "Jill wasn't that way."

"How do you know? When was the last time you saw her?"

"It's been a while."

"And you don't want to see her? I do not understand?"

"It's complicated."

He let it go with a shrug, mumbling about me going to see her. How could I explain the truth? There wasn't. With the rules WITSEC set in place, I was violating them plenty already. I didn't recall anything from a couple of weeks prior or drinking that much. I thought I was doing good holding in my tongue.

After polishing off the bottle, Manny staggered to his feet. We bid good night. He stumbled his way back to his camper on the far edges of the campground.

I switched on the television and began packing away the medic pack. The local news came on and the news anchor mentioned Torrance County, New Mexico. I stopped what I was doing.

The scene shifted. There was Musgrave's ranch, old, faded, and rundown. It still looked the same it had when Logan and I had been there. But then Thomas's house popped up. I saw the hell and carnage Logan had lived through. It had been almost two years since that night. The house looked ready to fall in on itself from the looks of it. The news anchor rattled on.

"*Inside this house, five people were brutally gunned down…*" For the next few minutes, the investigative reporter went into a detailed spiel about what happened or what he thought happened. The news reporter wanted to know why the law enforcement community was remaining silent on the topic. But the main man at the center of the report was, of all people, Logan Pierce. The segment focused on his involvement. They were angling that somehow he was some high-roller gangster like the infamous Mexican drug kingpin *El Chapo.* They also pointed out the possibility he was hiding within the WITSEC program, living the high life off taxpayer funds. None of that was close to being true.

Anyone on this side of WITSEC would've told them you get a small monthly allowance, enough to kick start your new life, but no one was getting big dollars.

There was no mention of my name, my old name. The whole segment centered on Logan. Perhaps that made me a bit jealous. After all, it was my idea to go after the money. You'd think the news would lend me a tiny fragment of credit or something. Logan was the main man and always had been since this mess first blew up. The segment ended with the words: "*...it's a silent mystery, one that New Mexicans and those involved may never know the truth.*"

I popped the top on a can of PBR and took a deep swallow. I stepped outside, lit up a smoke. I studied the distant deep blue -red skies of the setting sun. The breeze kicked up, caressing my face with the hot winds flowing across the desert and with it, the stench of hydrogen sulfide. Gas flares burned at the numerous well sites, tearing holes in the fabrics of the darkness.

"A mystery," I muttered. *My whole damned life is a stinking mystery.*

I pulled the picture of Jill from my battered wallet. I studied it for a long time, thinking about the things that could've been.

FIFTEEN

I got back into the rock-n-roll of the oil fields. Along with the mundane duty of oil changes, I stayed busy performing complex jobs like rebuilding engines, clutch jobs, rebuilding suspension system by day. At night, I chased broken machines scattered all across the field. I still had Ricardo by my side. We took the beatings in stride. The company, being the pricks they were, refused to hire anyone else to help fix the shit-piles of rolling junk.

On the upside, the single silver lining of hope, we were being forced to take a single day off a week. Upper management back in Huston made it seem like they cared but there was an underlying motive in forcing us to take one day off. It was about the money. Both of us were working an average of ninety to a hundred and five hours a week. On top of that, we were ordering thousands of dollars in parts. Bottom line? We were cutting pretty heavy into their bottom line.

I chose Saturdays while Ricardo chose Sundays for religious reasons. While on my downtime, I usually stayed in the camper. I read, watched movies, cleaned and scrubbed the trailer down to kill the boredom, or worse, drank a shit-ton of booze. Sometimes I traveled around town or on up to Kermit. They offered better food options and a wide choice of pawnshops. There were plenty of tools floating around in the pawnshops. I could always use more heavy iron on the service truck.

I bought an old 9mm Browning Hi-Power at one pawn shop. I was surprised I passed the background check. I figured the Marshals would've placed a hold on that but the paperwork went through with no issues. A few weeks later, I bought a High Standard K1200 12 gauge. I had seen enough rattlesnakes in the field and felt packing a shotgun in the service truck might be a good idea. A twelve-gauge was overkill, but I hated snakes enough to justify it.

On other days of the month, I had to make a run to Fort Stockton to meet up with my counselor. The Marshals still wanted to keep tabs on me. After several months, they saw, or felt, I was finally adjusting to my new life. Perhaps I was, but I still felt I was a mystery the world would never know. The counseling sessions eventually dropped off to meeting only once every few months. I was fine with that. I hated fighting all the traffic driving down Highway 285.

I continued to stay busy even as the Hyperion Oil ship was sinking.

Word was around the campfire was that Hyperion was sinking by the day. Looking around the yard, I figured the statement was coming to fruition. Most of the big dog oil companies weren't calling Hyperion to haul their oil. It wasn't just the equipment was torn to bits. It had more to do with management making promises they couldn't keep.

Eventually, the day came everyone was dreading. After busting my ass for Hyperion for the better part of eighteen months, it all came to an end. I had been out in the field all night chasing broken trucks and finally had time to roll back into the yard. It was just in time for a big meeting. Hyperion could no longer sustain itself financially and they were shutting it down as of noon the next day.

I didn't know whether to feel relief or anger, which some of the newer drivers felt. It was easy to understand why. Most of them had given up everything to be here in the oilfields. They had left families, their old jobs in the hopes of making the big bucks. Most hadn't even managed to stuff away first paychecks.

I drove the service truck back to camp not sure what to feel or think. I guess I was numb about it all. I started cleaning and organizing things around the camper. I had to make plans and moving might be one of those plans. I took a long look. The air conditioner hummed. There were piles of beer cans and some old leftover food lying on the table and counters. I had gotten slack on cleaning.

I started going through an old bag I had carted around with me since I began my odyssey a couple of years ago. The bag had stayed stuffed away in the corner of the trailer since I put it there months ago. I decided it was time to shuffle things around and toss a few things. I pulled out a pair of shirts and heard a jingle and clatter of something metallic hit the floor. I paused, looked down. I caught my breath and saw it was a key. The inscription of letters gleamed under the light.

NNRR.

The key had been stuffed away in one of my old shirt pockets. I picked it up off the floor and held it to the light. Twirling it slowly around the fingertips, I became lost in my thoughts. I had been a rich man once, a little over a quarter million richer than I was at that moment. Jill and I had made plans. There was talk of marriage, talk about moving to California, settling down, setting up a retirement fund, everything. The keyword was *'had'*. Would she have even stuck around once the money had run out? That was a troublesome thought. When I got the money, I was determined to make it count toward retirement.

I hadn't saved anything for retirement. In late 1991, I opted out of the military. Maybe that was a bad move. I could've been retired by now. But at the time, I didn't want anything more to do with the Army. I wasted a few months boozing and chasing broads much against my wife's wishes. We divorced and she got what little money we had left. After a while, I told myself I better get moving on rebuilding a retirement along with a career.

The career path was easy enough. I took up the wrench and studied for a career as a diesel mechanic. The career counselor at the community college tried talking me out of it. She wanted me in the medical program saying it was a better fit. But to be honest, I didn't want to deal with the blood and shit either.

The retirement path was different. Every company I swore to retire from went belly up, got bought out by a competitor, or the benefit packages dwindled to nothing. Eventually, by the mid-2000s, there wasn't a company left worth their salt in paying a working man a retirement or offering a decent 401k plan. Sure, the union gigs were still around but after the economic turmoil in 2008, even they were looking to cut the pensions out of the picture to maintain their astronomical profit lines.

Holding the key in my hand, I thought about what could've been, what might've been, and the possibilities. Where would I have been if I still had that damned money?

Could've been, should've been, and might've been....it doesn't solve the problem.

I booted up the laptop, signed on, and cracked open a cold

one. I made a mental note to only drink down a couple of brews.

It had been a couple of years now. Things should've calmed down. The money was no longer a bone of contention or concern for anybody except the local police and the Federal alphabet agencies involved. The first search results for Jill had come back with nothing. Not unusual. I checked up on her alternate name, her maiden name, Monroe. It came back with one result and showed she worked at Stubby's Grocery store as a cashier in Estancia. Checking her stats, I saw she was single. There were no pictures of her. Her main photo was a group of yellow flowers glowing under the sun.

I took up a pen and scribbled a few notes. I had an idea of where she was. I debated for a bit, mulling the idea of shooting her a message but nixed it. It would be better if I talked to her in person. Leaning back in the seat, I gave it careful thought. If I did go and see her, what would her response be?

We hadn't spoken for months and there hadn't been any attempt to communicate. I thought about trying a few times but I would've had to go through the channels set in place by the US Marshals. If they even approved of such a request. But if I took some time off and went to see her on my own? That could work, but I had to take precautions. A very strict set of precautions.

I had lived in Moriarty for the better part of six years and knew a lot of people. It was also ground zero where the Dixie Mafia and the missing money scandal took place. In reality, I could've cared less about the money. I'd stack a mountain with all the money in the world and set it to flames to see Jill again. Maybe there was a slim chance to convince her in coming back here to Texas with me. I knew she would if I just had a chance to talk to her.

Or was I lying to myself trying to keep a single ember alive in the aftermath of a vast fire?

I shoved the fantasy aside. I began a search for Logan and

Amy. Amy hadn't given a clue one of Logan's new name or where they were living. She didn't trust me. She was right.

I typed in her name. *Ava Williams.*

I cleared out the browser history for a second time and signed back onto Facebook. The Marshals frowned heavily on the use of any social media platform. I could see their point. It was too easy for people to find you when you least expected it and sometimes, it might not be for the best reasons. But, when you look around for people on social media, it's a fairly simple process. It takes some time, but if a person is persistent, they will eventually trip across what they're looking for.

I searched various combinations for Williams, Ava, anything. Nothing came back as anything positive. Amy wasn't going to have anything to do with any social platform. She was a stickler on adhering to the rules. It dawned on me. If I was using a fake profile, it could be assured Logan was using one too. I tried combinations of words. Anything related to diesel mechanics and the name Williams. I tossed in Peterbilts, truck stops, dealerships, and Chevrolet into the search. Logan was a big-time Chevy man.

Sidney, Montana showed a promising hit. I was sure of it. Larry Williams. He was working at a dealership. The crucial key was in the profile picture. It was a pair of hands holding onto each other and the familiar ring on one of the digits. Amy had given Logan the ring, and he wore it on a necklace. Now it was on her finger. I recognized Amy's hand due to the small scar at the base of the thumb. Logan's hand was rough-looking and showed faded grease stains. At least the mystery was solved. They were still together. I knew where they lived.

I took the chance and shot him a message hoping for a response. Eventually, an hour and two beers later, he answered. Of course, he denied it was him. That pussy. I took a picture of the key in my hand. I told him I knew where the money was. I lied about the money, of course, but I wanted to see what the response would be.

I waited for an answer, but Logan never answered. I waited a long time, smoking one cigarette after another. The cell phone went off like an explosion in the silence. I grabbed it, half-expecting the number to pop up to be Logan, but found it was dispatch from Hyperion.

"This George," I said

"Got one for you," the voice sounded tired, bored. "A simple road call."

"Mike," I said, "You know this is all over? Hyperion is finished? Bankrupt?"

"I'm sure this is the last one for all of us," the sound of computer keyboard keys tapped in the background. "I got Rubin broke down at the Dogleg site. Something about a bad air leak and can't move off the pad. Manny is lined up behind him too, waiting to load. You up for it?"

I closed the laptop. Hyperion was still operational for a few hours. I could grab what money was left and stay on the clock until noon. "Yeah, why not?"

SIXTEEN

The Dogleg well site was some fifteen miles back into the interior of no man's land. No one was sure if it was on the Texas side or the New Mexico side. Hence the term No Man's Land. The lone battery of oil silos pumped out so little oil, it took only two loads of crude out every twenty-four hours. The hard part was navigating the trails leading to it. I knew the area well enough though. The Chevy navigated through dips and rises, or the occasional sandpit until the lights from Dogleg came into view in the distance.

I rolled up on the pad and trapped within the beams of the Chevy's headlights, Manny and Rubin wandered out of the shadows. Rolling to a stop, Manny tossed out a casual greeting.

"*Amigo*!" he shouted. "Get this guy off the pad already."

I snickered, popped the door open, and grabbed my flashlight.

"Where's the leak coming from?"

Rubin wandered up. "Somewhere under the trailer."

"Could be an airline, an airbag...hopefully, an airline though."

Rubin shrugged. "It's yours to take care of."

I knelt behind the tanker trailer. The airbags were still inflated. "Okay, it's not the airbags. Go release the trailer brakes."

I didn't see Rubin moving. I shot a look up at him. He had to have heard what I said to do. Rubin clutched a pistol in his hand. "What the…?" I was sure it was a joke. "Is there a snake?" I looked around.

Rubin winced. "No joke.

A minute passed, my smile turned to a frown. I had no idea what was going on. Manny stood off to my right by the service truck, hands still jammed in his windbreaker. "Manny?"

He wasn't moving and his face wore a serious expression.

"It's no joke, my friend," Rubin shook his head.

I held my hands up. "What's this about?"

Rubin was silent. The gun was pointed at my stomach. The only answer was from the sound of the flare roaring nearby. I did the only natural thing to do in this kind of situation. I bolted. If I made it to the Chevy, I had the twelve-gauge resting in the back of the cab. I didn't know what was going on but I had to do something.

I got to the service truck, jerked the door open, lunged inside, fingers fumbled for the shotgun. Just as I reached for it, my mind registered it was gone.

"*Amigo*," a voice called out to my right. I turned just in time to meet the butt-end of my shotgun. A few hard thumps across my face and I crumpled to the ground. A few kicks were thrown in for good measure, knocking the wind out of me. I rolled around on the dusty ground in pain. A pair of rough hands grabbed me by the shirt. I was hoisted up to my feet and thrown against the service truck. More hard punches. I fell again to the ground.

I held up my arms warding off the worst of the blows. Manny whispered that I had enough and Rubin backed away. Through the dusty air, Manny knelt in front of me. The shotgun lay across his legs. "This is not what we wish."

"You gotta hell of a way of showing that!" I spat.

Manny looked up to Rubin and gave a nod. Rubin reached into his jacket. Clutched in his hand was a manila folder. He held it out.

"Take it," Manny whispered.

"Fuck you, Manny," I gave both of them the best look of defiance I could. "Fuck the both of you!"

Manny grabbed two fistfuls of my shirt and shook violently. "Listen! You take the envelope and look! You should have listened to me and left to go back to Moriarty to see your woman! It was a hint! But now we have to resort to this."

I was puzzled. "Why in hell would I do that?"

"I don't know," he spat. "We are told to do this." He looked over and gave Rubin a nod.

Rubin held out the envelope.

I reached up and took hold of it. Rubin let go of his end and stepped back. "We're sorry, George, we are. We're just messengers in this."

I felt confused. "Messengers?"

Manny nodded. "Messengers, that is all we are," he looked at the envelope. "Open it."

Breathing hard and with trembling fingers, I tore the end open on the envelope. I shook out two photos within. Manny stood up and stepped back. I took up one photo. It was me, long, graying hair. On the back of the photo was the ink stamping. In bold red letters stating it was the property of the US Marshals. The other photograph showed Jill. I knew it was her just by the shape of her figure and the red-hair.

I shot Manny a look. "You mother fucker, you wouldn't."

"We don't know anything about this. We do as we're told."

Rubin nodded in agreement. "It's true, please do not take this personally," he swallowed hard. "It is business."

"Business?" I snarled. "To threaten me? With this shit?"

Manny ignored the comment. "*Llaves*," he said to Rubin. Rubin reached into his pocket and produced a key. He tossed it to the ground at my feet.

Manny continued. "You'll take this key and go back to Moriarty. From there, you will wait in the motel room until someone contacts you."

"The fuck I will," I held my arm up, half-expecting him to kick, but he didn't.

"Then you forfeit this woman's life. Is this what you want? After everything you have told us about how much you miss her?"

"No," I muttered.

Rubin held out a hand. "We're sorry for this, but you must go back to Moriarty."

I hesitated, expecting to get nailed again, but Manny stepped back further to give the appearance that nothing more was going to happen unless I acted up. He was still clutching my shotgun. "Get up."

I took hold of Rubin's offering. I stood up on wobbling legs. Rubin tried to help steady my wobbling, but I shook him off. My trust in him was destroyed. I leaned against the service truck. Its surface felt good. I leaned over, still feeling the heavy throbs hammering my guts.

Manny stood against the backdrop of the flare. His dark shadow menacing, evil-looking. Rubin was cast in the same light. I staggered to the open driver-side door and slid in behind the wheel with gritted teeth. Rubin closed the door. He leaned in. "You have but twenty-four hours to get there."

"What the fuck is in this for you? Money? Dope? What? I fucking trusted you guys. Who are you working for?" I looked at him with a hard glare.

He stayed silent only looking back to Manny, and then back to me. "Some very powerful people in Mexico who have vested interest."

"Mexico?"

"It is all I can say, *amigo*."

"The fucking Cartel? Which one?"

He didn't answer and I couldn't read his face, but there was worry etched in the mask of toughness. "I have a cousin. Her name is Erika. You will know her. The people we work for have her."

"Have her?" I was confused.

"You will figure it out, George, but..." he bit his lower lip. "Make sure nothing happens to her. It is all I ask."

"Wait...you guys beat my ass and then expect me to help you?" I chuckled. "You got another thing coming." I looked at Manny and stuck my hand out, holding up the middle finger. "And fuck you too!" I flipped the selector in reverse. The Chevy peeled out in a cloud of dust. I slammed the selector down into drive and spun around. The sound of tools and parts slammed around the interior of the truck and the utility bed. I didn't care. I wanted off the site to figure this mess out. I aimed the Chevy off the pad and hauled ass into the thick darkness.

SEVENTEEN

The hour-long drive back to the man-camp was silent. My brain was roaring with thoughts of every kind. Everything from outright murder, which the Marshals would frown upon, to just packing and running. What to do? I pulled up to the camp and killed the ignition. The sound of silence flooded the cab. All that could be heard was my heavy breathing. The exterior light behind my camper swayed, casting shadows of doubt. If I didn't do anything, Jill was dead. If I called the Marshals, Jill was dead. If I didn't get to the motel, Jill was dead. Every avenue of escape always led to Jill getting murdered.

I grabbed the photo of Jill off the passenger seat. The photo was recent, may be taken within the last few months. There was nothing marked on the back of the picture. I grabbed the other picture of me, flipped it over, and read the back of it again. The US Marshal's rubber stamp pissed me off to no end.

"Mother fuckers!" I slammed a meaty hand on the steering wheel. "Fuck!" I wondered how in hell, the Cartel had managed to get that photograph. I drew a blank, not wanting to assume the worst. But it was the only logical choice.

Someone within the Marshals had sold me out. The question was who? I felt I knew who to blame, but there was no solid proof.

I took the key, looked hard at the inscription on the brown, plastic tag.

Zia RV and Motel. The address was faded but still legible.

I crammed it in my pocket, scooped up the photos, and popped the door open. The warm night breeze that often washed away the heat of the day hit me. The wind picked up in tempo. The kind of storm that dominated the open deserts of the southwest. I lit up a smoke, stepped out, groaning a hiss through thin lips. Once inside the camper, I turned on the light in the bathroom and started cleaning up the battle damage off my face. I felt like I'd done a few rounds with Mike Tyson. It still irked me the two bastards got over on me.

I spent several minutes cleaning up. Besides the cut above my eye and the bangs and bruises, everything was going to be fine besides the feelings part. Running the shower, I got cleaned up and threw on a set of civilian duds.

I lit up another smoke, stepped outside on the makeshift porch, watching the last of the desert storm blow itself out. The summer night was a relief. In a few hours, oilfield life would start. The town and the oil field workers were going to be clogging the roads and gas stations.

I had it all planned out at one point. I liked working in the oilfields. It was going to be a pain in the ass having to leave it all. The challenges were always present and kept my attention focused. I could always come back to a different outfit. Hell, everyone was looking for mechanics and truck drivers. The Marshals were going to be suspicious in time. I figured a few days before they caught on to the fact I was roaming around in forbidden territory. By then I might be dead.

I looked around, contemplating my options. I knew what to do but were my balls big enough? The whole key was keeping Jill alive. There was no other option. *Rubin mentioned his cousin...what was her name? Erika...* She might hold a key to the puzzle, maybe. I looked at the time on the cell phone.

0337.

My mind was focused on a plan. I didn't know who all the players were, not yet, but I'd resigned myself to the fact that if Jill was in trouble, I'd go back to prevent anything happening to her or her family. I stepped into the camper, shutting the door behind me. I knelt by the vent on the floor. I worked the screws loose, lifted the cover, jammed a hand in the vent, and pulled out a plastic baggy. Within was all my old paperwork.

I had a few name changes along the way courtesy of the US Marshals. The Marshals always wanted all the old paperwork back with each name change. The reasons were obvious. I gave them the old stuff they had issued originally, but I made duplicates of each identity. One never knew when such items might come in handy.

I packed my old duffel bag with a change of clothes. I tossed the Browning on top of the pile. I packed the medic kit and computer in the bag before cinching down the drawstrings.

I'd thought about taking the service truck but nixed it. All company trucks had tracking devices. A few more had onboard camera systems. I didn't need to explain to the head man of Hyperion why his service truck was out of the area.

I shouldered the bag, opened the camper door. The cool morning air felt good. The bus depot was a half-mile away. There would be a bus headed to Roswell, New Mexico. I'd catch a second one to Albuquerque.

The moon hung silently in the sky. I moved through the campgrounds, out to the main highway to the bus depot. The depot was dingy, dark with a single neon sign that sputtered and buzzed over the main entrance. I made a bee-line to the gift shop and bought a phone. I then bought a one-way ticket to Roswell under my old name Alan Moore.

EIGHTEEN

The 203-mile marker lay just ahead along the long stretch of I-40. The young woman seated next to me had thankfully fallen asleep. For most of the trip, she yapped about going to Hollywood. She was from some shit-kicker town in Georgia. She wanted to make it big in the movie industry. I figured she'd be doing porn flicks within a few months. Along the way, I worked mentally on a plan. None of the plans were playing out to any good, but still, any plan was better than none. I took my bag, stood up, and walked up the swaying aisle. I plopped down behind the bus driver.

"I need off at the next exit," I stated.

The driver stole a glance. "Here?"

"Yes, please."

"There won't be a refund or pro-rate, you understand, sir?"

"I do."

The driver shook his head but steered off I-40. The bus rolled up the exit ramp then stopped just before the stop sign. He pulled on a lever and the doors hissed open allowing the hot summer air to flood in. Stepping off the bus, I took a deep breath. The doors slapped shut before roaring off in a cloud of diesel and dust. The cumbersome beast glided over the road, down the on-ramp, and back on the freeway.

Distant thunderheads rolled across the Estancia valley, dragging wide, thick rain funnels behind them. The occasional jolt of lightning tore through the dense fabric of moisture, striking the ground like God was cauterizing an open wound. Rain clouds swept over Moriarty giving those living under the clouds a mild reprieve from the worst of the summer heat.

Glancing behind me, just over the overpass, the familiar wooden structure of the 203 strip club still stood. A few semi-trucks were parked in the adjacent lot along with a few local cars and old farm trucks. Ahead stood the RV Park and Motel.

I walked to the RV Park situated just a hundred or so yards away. Walking under the arched sign, the letters were faded and peeling paint. The Zia RV Park and Motel was nothing more than a shadow of its former self.

Thick plumes of waist-high weeds, mixed with garbage and tumbleweeds were piled high against the wooden fence surrounding the property. I was glad to be back in familiar territory. It was a strange feeling I took as an omen, a good one.

The RV Park was dilapidated, run-down, worn. Only the road running through the park was cleared of weeds and debris. There was one other camper on site. All the other lots were empty, overgrown from lack of use. The motel part of the compound was constructed from chalky white broken cinder blocks with plenty of cracks and peeling plaster. Some of the rooms were taped off with old yellow tape laced across the doorways. There were no other occupants.

I walked by an old blue Chevy truck parked along the pathway. The main building had a small sign in bright painted lettering stating it was the main office. An old man was waging war with the weeds with nothing more than a machete and it was clear the weeds were winning. I walked slowly up to the old man, who had his back turned to me. I cleared my throat to get his attention. He turned slowly, his watery ancient blues eyes widened in surprise.

"Huh?"

I held up a hand, keeping an eye on the machete. "You guys open for business?"

The machete wobbled in his creased hand. "Oh, you a potential customer?" He didn't wait for an answer, turned, and cried out, "Margie!"

An older woman, perhaps older than the man, waddled to the doorway of the building. "Help you?"

"Looking for a room," I held up the motel key. "Number sixteen?"

She opened the door and stepped out. "You the man who rented the room for a week?"

"I guess I did."

She nodded. "C'mon in and fill out some paperwork," she held the door open and I walked through. "You paid already but we still need some paperwork done."

The old man went back to waging his war with the weeds.

I stepped into the lounge area, waited a moment for my eyes to adjust before walking over to the counter. "So it's paid for?"

Margie was small, thin, and ancient-looking, "You did pay upfront, remember?" she giggled softly.

"I guess I did," I set my duffel bag down. "Sorry, I've been moving town to town. I forget which ones I pay for upfront." Whoever wanted me here planned on me staying for a week and paid upfront? I was curious who the main player was.

The foray was small, nothing much was notable. The walls were lined with black and white pictures, some color but all were from the old days when the RV Park and motel had better times. "How long?"

"How long what?"

"Have you been in business?"

"Oh," she thought for a moment. "Since about 1964. Have you been here before?"

"No, I've driven by and always wanted to stop in." There was no point in admitting I had lived around here before.

"Things haven't been the same since the housing market crashed a few years ago." She held up a finger, pointing to a table. "Can you hand me that stack of papers?"

I stepped over, scooped up the papers, and handed them to her. She quickly began running her fingers through the forms, picked one out, and handed it to me. "If you could fill this out for me."

I took it and began filling it out. "So things changed?"

"Everything. You know some people just up and left their homes? I mean, just up and left, moved away. I guess they couldn't afford the housing around here even though it was cheap." She looked over out the nearby window. "We're just barely hanging on ourselves."

"That's a shame," I replied. I took out my wallet, opened it, and thumbed through the bills within. "I noticed you had an old Chevy pickup outside in the weeds."

She looked over my shoulder. I followed her gaze. The Chevy was a late seventies long bed. The blue paint had faded down to the primer and where the primer had worn through. The rusty patches ate away on the bare metal. "That jalopy's been sitting there for the last couple of years. Harold, bless his heart, can't drive anymore. The State took away his license."

"So, does it run?"

"Harold starts it every other day or so."

I thumbed through the bills within my wallet. "I'd like to borrow it for a couple of days?" I placed a couple of one hundred dollar bills on the counter.

"I don't know. Harold is attached to that thing."

I placed another two hundred on the growing pile. "I promise I'll take care of it. I need a ride to a couple of places around here."

She looked back at the ledger. "It'll be fine, mister...*ahhh*?" she questioned.

I slid my driver's license over the counter. "Moore, Alan Moore, mam."

"The keys for the truck are in the ignition."

"Harold won't mind?"

She smiled. "He was planning on selling it anyway. I don't think he'll mind if someone borrows it in the meantime."

She scooped up the bills, and they disappeared under her apron. She copied the information off the driver's license and handed over a receipt. I tucked the scrap of paper in my pocket.

I started for the door and had just pushed it open.

"You never did say if business or pleasure?"

I held the door and gave a thin smile. "Pleasure...I hope."

NINETEEN

The room was down on the far end of the complex. The concrete walkway was in bad shape, cracked and slabs lifted. If one wasn't careful, they could easily trip, fall or the worse get a stubbed toe.

I unlocked the door, nudged it open, and felt a wave of cool air rush. I expected to be met by the person or persons who demanded my audience to be here, but no one was in the room. I shut the door and looked around for a moment. The first rule of thumb was to check out everything first. Not only had the Army taught me the skill but the US Marshals had pounded it into my lessons.

The ac unit hummed in the window, the bed was made, clean and sharp. The dresser and bedside table gleaned from a coat of fresh polish. The bathroom was all true vintage seventies fixtures but clean, presentable. A clouded privacy window was just above the toilet. The window slid up nice and easy. Poking my head out, I saw the drop was nothing. It was nice to have a second way out just in case.

Satisfied, I returned to the main room, tossed my duffel bag down at the foot of the bed, and plopped down on the edge. I made a call to Stubby's Grocery store in Estancia and asked for Jill. The woman on the other end of the line sounded bored.

"Can I speak to Jill, please?"

"May I ask whose calling?"

"A friend with a quick question."

"She's busy in the back, if you like, I can take a message?"

"What time does she get off?"

"We close at ten, sir."

"No way to talk to her? It's rather important."

The woman sighed. "Can you hold?"

"Sure."

The phone went to hold, beeping a couple of times. I pressed the end button on my phone. At least there was solid confirmation Jill was working up until ten o'clock. The Cartel hadn't messed with her as of yet. I glanced down at the time on the phone.

6:18

I still had time to kill. I went back into the bathroom. Looking up at the ceiling, I saw the tiles. Just like the old days in the military, I learned you have to hide things you don't want to have stolen. Cheap motels like the Zia were not immune from theft. Standing on the toilet, I shoved one aside. It was a perfect niche in which to hide the computer and pistol. After stowing away the things I didn't want to be stolen or lost, I went back into the room, flopped back on the bed, and waited for Manny and Rubin's Cartel buddies

TWENTY

The Chevy bounced. Every time the machine inched anywhere close to the forty-five-mile-per-hour mark, the front end felt like it was going to give out. It was bearable, but it was proving to be more than an annoyance. The day's heat dissipated with the sinking of the sun. The cool breeze rushing through the windows felt good. I smoked my Marlboro thinking of my next move.

I got tired of waiting. I needed a beer. Whoever wanted me here was just going to have to wait a bit. I left a note taped to the door stating I was on a beer run and I'd be back. But I had other plans in the mix.

I cruised into Moriarty via the frontage road observing all the changes that had occurred during my absence. I was apprehensive about going into town at all. The feeling was something like when I first landed in Saudi Arabia back in '90 for Desert Shield. I didn't have any idea of what kind of war to expect. No one did really. All we knew was we were building up to something big, something violent. The Iraqi Army wasn't budging an inch out of Kuwait. We knew we were going to be putting the might of the US military boot right up their ass soon.

Moriarty though? I knew what had happened here. Everyone living here sure remembered. Was the Dixie Mafia still floating around? The Cartel was. That was a definite.

Duggan's Truck Stop was now known as the County Line Truck Stop. That was a strange name. The Torrance County line was about seven miles down further west on I-40. Business looked the same but had the people changed? It was a given that nothing stays the same in terms of help. There might be one or two people from the old regime but I was sure everyone I knew was long gone.

Truck stops the world over, all looked the same. Rows of trucks of all makes and models were lined up around the twenty-some-odd acre lot. Trucks rolled off I-40, turned, and lined up at the fuel pumps. Drivers walked to and from the main complex, either to rummage for grub from the restaurant or pay for fuel. The front of the main complex was lined with personal vehicles from the locals who thought dining at a truck stop made them part of the elite. I hated to tell people those days were a couple of decades dead. The old guard of drivers was slowly fading out and into the history books. The rough and tumble days of hard-core drivers were a rare breed to find.

My old hangout known as Pete's Bar was a sad reminder of the old days. Once a place for locals to meet and catch up on the town's gossip mill, weeds flourished around the cracked adobe building and the once-great local hangout sagged under its weight of an uncertain future. I pulled the Chevy into a parking spot in front of the bar and killed the ignition. The Chevy stalled and died with a series of protesting sputters.

I glanced down at the cell phone. The time was 7:22. I had plenty of time to grab a bite to eat, maybe a brew or two, grab that six-pack before pushing off back to the motel. Stepping out of the cab, I felt the gravel grind under my boots. The air stunk of burnt diesel and week-old trash. Locking the Chevy, I bounced in the main doors. I saw the local newspaper rack and dug around my pocket for a couple of quarters and grabbed a copy of the Mountain Telegraph before heading inside for a liquid diet.

Pete's Bar looked as run down on the inside as it did on the outside. The dark wooden floors were scuffed, worn from years of foot travel. The walls were covered in framed photos and rusty junk tidbits of the old days related to farming implements, or mounted deer heads and antlers. It took a minute for my eyes to adjust to the dark void. Several patrons were seated at nearby booths, old rancher types whose faces were carved deep of creases and wrinkles from years of exposure.

I took up a stool at the far end of the bar and ordered a beer. I took up the paper and read through the basic headlines. I realized things had changed in Moriarty in just two years. Besides the usual yap on local politics and county issues, there was talk of murder and burglary.

A man had been discovered dead in a vintage low rider Impala on the side of Highway 41. It looked like he had been pulled over by someone he knew and was shot. The clincher was he had worked here at the County Line Truck Stop. I didn't recognize the name, Diego Ramirez. I had worked at Duggan's for five years and knew everyone who had worked here during my tenure. This guy had come after Logan and I had long left the scene.

The article rambled on about how his family, recent immigrants from Mexico were searching and demanding answers while the Torrance County Sheriffs were saying the investigation was ongoing.

"Terrible thing."

I looked up and the blonde waitress smiled and slid the mug of beer in front of me.

"It sounds like it," I replied. I folded up the paper and set it aside.

"Yeah," she answered before setting down a cup of coffee, "I heard maybe a drug thing," she paused, scribbling down the order on a notepad. "I never expected that from Diego."

"You knew him?"

She snorted. "Everybody knew Diego."

"Well, if it's any consolation, my condolences," I said.

She waved off the statement. "No need, he was bad news as it was."

"How long had he been working over at the County Line?"

"Why? You a reporter?" She looked me over with furrowed eyebrows. "Maybe a private detective?"

"Neither. Just curious."

"A couple of years, right after the Duggan's Truck Stop chain were bought out."

"Who bought the Duggan's Truck Stop franchise?"

She shrugged. "Some rich cats from China I heard." Before I could ask any other questions, she changed the subject. "Whelp," she said. "If you need anything else, just holler." She spun away and went back to tending several other patrons who'd ordered another round of rot-gut.

I took up the paper again. I reread the article on the murder and found another article of interest. A woman had been missing now for close to two weeks. Erika Fernandez. She had disappeared after working a shift at the County Line Truck Stop as a waitress. Witnesses claimed she left work at around 1030 in the evening but had never made it home. Her car, a Toyota Highlander, was found a mile from her house on McNabb Road just south of Moriarty. The hood was propped open but she was nowhere to be found. Police speculated she had been kidnapped. The police didn't say how they came to that conclusion.

Erika Fernandez.

Rubin had said his cousin's name was Erika. Was this the same Erika? That would be too much of a coincidence but it couldn't be ruled out. The conclusion in my mind was that this was the same person. It also meant she might've been snagged by the Cartel. But for what reason I couldn't determine other than to leverage Rubin into forcing me into going back to Moriarty. Was there something more though?

I finished my beer in silent disgust, occasionally looking over the two articles again, memorizing every detail I could. I wasn't sure about the murder connection, but I couldn't rule it out either. The whole thing stank of Cartel, but there might be other players in the mix who were hiding in the shadows. The question was who?

I ordered a six-pack of beer to go, tossed a few bills on the counter, and headed back to the motel room with trouble on my mind. All I wanted to do was go back to the oilfields, hide, and hope this was nothing more than a bad dream. But here I was right back in the shit again when I didn't want to be. Jill was the only reason why I was here.

But the feeling about all the players who were involved kept scratching the back of my brain. The more I thought about it, the more concerning it all felt. For the first time in a long time, I felt a twinge of fear.

TWENTY-ONE

The motel room felt like a tomb. The air conditioner droned out a steady rhythm of cool air. The Three Stooges played on the television but the slap-stick did little to lift my spirits. When I arrived back at the motel, I half-expected someone to be here waiting for me, but there was no one. I was growing anxious about all the waiting time. Whoever wanted me here was sure taking their sweet-ass time getting here and I was growing more annoyed by the minute.

I rose off the bed, pulled the curtain aside. Nothing and nobody was outside. Old Harold and Marge had retired for the evening from their exhaustive warring offense on the weeds that grew all over the complex. The Chevy was parked outside. Its headlights wide open, begging me to go on a night run.

I knew Jill was working up until ten. Looking at the digital display on my phone, I had a little over an hour to get there. Once I got there, then what? I played and replayed so many different scenarios in my mind but none panned out or were too damn hokey to believe they would even come close to working.

I knew her first reaction would be an utter shock. That was a given. We hadn't seen each other in two years and there was too much lost time between us. But I still cared. That was my weakest link. Did she feel the same way though?

I let the curtain go. The outside world vanished from view. The last two years I spent chasing ruined dreams and hopes across a wasteland of doubt and perceived lost love. Would she even want me back after this debacle? Would she even understand that she was in true danger because of me?

"Oh...fuck it."

I scooped the keys off the bedside table, down the last bit of liquid courage before leaving the motel room. The note still hung on the door so if the people who wanted me here came looking, they would have to wait.

I fired off the Chevy and headed down Martinez Road toward Highway 41

.

TWENTY-TWO

Stubby's Grocery was just off the main drag in Estancia next to the Wells Fargo Bank. Just adjacent to the store was a small park overgrown with weeds and rusted playground equipment that the local kids didn't know how to use anymore. The rain had stopped long enough for the half-moon to poke through the silent gloom like God's angry toenail.

I was trying to decide on the best approach, running a constant stream of scenarios in my mind. The bigger question would be if she listened to my explanations or called the Marshals. She had sold me out once before. If she just gave me a few minutes, I knew I could talk her into listening to first. No matter how many times I rehearsed it over the past hour, I couldn't decide. It had been almost two years since I had seen her. My heart was racing.

I sat parked in the furthest part of the damp lot. The lot next door was an old bar. It was already closed for the night but someone had forgotten to shut off the red neon sign glowing overhead. The sign flickered and flashed off and on, splashing a hellish haze of soft red over the parking lot and the hood of the Chevy. I sat under the flashing glow, eyes intently watching the employees spill out of the doors, talking, laughing, while a tall man in a white smock overcoat locked the doors to the store.

Several vehicles were scattered across the lot. I assumed all belonged to the employees. I wasn't sure which one belonged to Jill. The red Durango I bought her was nowhere to be seen. I wondered if the Feds had confiscated it. The rest of the vehicles were newer model trucks and a burgundy Ford sedan.

And then I saw her.

Jill was still slender, long legs clad in tight jeans with a loose-fitting blouse. She wore white tennis shoes. Her silent footfalls traipsed across the asphalt lot ever so closely. I reached for the door handle, my mind on automatic. But just as my fingertips touched the handle, the Ford truck parked halfway down fired off, a tall man got out. His western hat was down low over his eyes, concealing his dark features. I looked back at Jill. I could see a wide smile stretched across her face.

I watched them kiss and laugh. Jill slid inside the passenger seat. The driver jumped back behind the steering wheel. The truck lurched into gear and sped off through the parking lot. Thick smoke followed in its wake. They hung a sharp left out onto the streets before disappearing from view.

I sat alone in the dark cab, watching the gauzy exhaust smoke floating lazily across the windshield. My hopes were dashed on the rocky formations of gut-wrenching truth. Gone were my thoughts about Jill and I ever hooking up again. Gone were the looming threats of the Cartel. I wished I hadn't seen her. I wished I hadn't bothered waiting here. I regretted ever going on this God-damned venture. I cursed the people who drug me here to Moriarty.

I fired up the Chevy with numb fingers, slid it into gear, and headed back to Moriarty.

TWENTY-THREE

I hit the 203 strip club right on 80's night. The other bars around town were closing up, and other bar options were slim at best. I thought about going to Albuquerque but scratched the idea. I didn't want to risk getting a little carried away with the booze. I was in the mood to quench the flames of mistrust and deceit.

The place was jammed-packed. Locals dressed up in what they thought were eighties duds while the ever-present topless broads roamed around looking for the sugar-daddy willing to part with his next dollar.

The Eurythmics tune *Love is a Stranger* thumped from the speakers while a long-haired blonde danced on the center stage. Her well-tanned figure twisted and twirled to the beat before a small crowd of truck drivers who tossed down the occasional dollar bill at her feet. I wasn't paying any attention. My mind was elsewhere.

I was busy downing the last of my second shot of Jack and coke by the time the stage lit up. A couple of broads, a bleached blonde, and a black-haired raven slid out on stage for the next set. Frankie Goes to Hollywood's *Relax* exploded from the sound system.

I ordered a round of Old Milwaukee and thought what the hell to do next. With Jill out of the picture love-wise, it was easy to move around now. I didn't give two-shits about the Cartel. Maybe it was the booze whispering sweet nothings in my brain, but I didn't care about the Marshals selling me out to the Cartel either.

Jesus, what the fuck was I thinking anyway? I thought. My brain was slogging through another barrage of scenarios. I should just hop on a bus to anywhere and get out of here. Anywhere other than here sounded good but then Jill was still in danger. I frowned. I took another swallow of beer.

And then what? I thought. The Cartel would have a hey-day kidnapping, torturing, and murdering her and her family. No way could I live with that on my conscience.

"You look lonely, stranger."

I looked over. She was a slender, small, petite woman with blonde hair and large brown eyes. She was leaning over the bar, looking into my eyes. She wore tight faded jeans with a loose-fitting red blouse with those large sleeve ruffles no one has seen since the eighties. Her thoughtful gaze transmitted trouble in waves of silent screams.

I hadn't realized anyone had gotten close. "No, not really," I said

"It's a party and you don't look like you're into it," she leaned in closer, "I thought maybe you were lonely."

"Thanks, I'm fine."

"Do you party?"

I looked over to the stage where the broads were dancing themselves silly. "It's strange a gal like you being here."

"Why not? This is the only bar in town still open at this time of night."

"You into strippers?" It was an unusual question but some broads go to strip clubs for a variety of reasons.

She hid a smile in her glass, took a deep swallow. "Wouldn't you like to know," she held out her hand. "I'm Paula."

I took hold of her soft hand, smiled. I ditched the name, Alan Moore. I had taken my old driver's license. "I'm George."

"George..." her voice trailed off.

I nodded, waved my hand in understanding. "I know I get that a lot."

She gripped my arm and laughed. "I didn't mean it that way."

Something was ripping my gut, telling me to leave Moriarty, tonight, like right now, but this woman had a hold on me. Why not experience one last fling before heading off into the sunset? I pushed aside the notion of leaving into the cloud of alcohol vapors. "What about this party?"

TWENTY-FOUR

I can't tell you what happened. Somewhere between the blurs of laughing faces, half-nude women, and angry shouts from men, life got smeared over within the thick gauze of alcoholic fumes. I danced, I drank, and eventually, as it sometimes happens, there was a fight. That was all I could surmise.

Paula hung on my arm, laughing and having a good time but sometime late in the early morning hours, she disappeared. I didn't care either. There were plenty of other broads. Several men, truck drivers, you could always tell them apart from the normal civilians, were yelling and tossing dollar bills on the stage. Some words were exchanged and we went to war. It was probably over nothing but it meant something at the time.

The bar bouncers came running, rough hands grabbed a hold, and out the door I went. I brushed myself off, took a good hard look at the Chevy. Then there was the Torrance County deputy parked across the road, hidden within the trees. I nixed the idea of driving. Zia RV Park was just across the bridge.

Hell, I could walk that.

I staggered off, cursing Paula. I could have bedded her down easily. All she had to do was wait just a bit longer. I wondered if she took off with another guy. That would seem my luck tonight. First Jill, now Paula.

I made it over the overpass when my gut started to revolt. The sounds of traffic on I-40 rushed under the bridge. It was an easy fifty yards from the Zia RV arched framework. My gut said to take a detour into the weeds. I retched, gagged, fell over, and vomited a long, hard stream of hot stew. Once the dry heaves had subsided, I staggered back up to the bridge and sat down. The night air felt good. Groaning, I fell back against the bridge railing. My eyes were heavy. A pair of headlights glared out. Shadows of booted feet clobbering the asphalt came into view just in front of the glaring lights. I didn't give two-flips for anything. The world went black.

TWENTY-FIVE

The world wobbled on a lopsided axis. There was the sound of something chopping the air, like a helicopter rotor. A brief image spilled out of my memory. A Huey UH-1 medivac had landed, kicking up a cloud of golden dust. I was working on a guy, elbows deep in blood, trying to keep the soldier alive. His young face filled with wide eyes. The fear carved deep in them, pleading for me to keep him alive. His mouth worked out a scream, but all he managed was a rush of air from his lungs. The image faded, and I opened one sticky eyelid. A ceiling fan spun overhead.

I tried moving a hand but felt tight resistance and the sound of a chain rattling. I tried moving again and saw the handcuffs linked from my wrist to the bedpost above my head.

I wondered if Paula had returned, scooped me up, and was into some kinky bondage stuff but after looking down, I was still wearing my clothes. Disappointed, I looked around. The room was small. The walls were painted in an ancient yellow mustard color. There was nothing extravagant in terms of furniture. A worn-out dresser, a side table with a chair next to it, and the bed I was lying in. I started to panic, yanking hard at the handcuffs holding me down.

"Hey," The voice drew my attention to a man in the corner. At least I thought it was a corner.

"Hey, Erin!" The shadow in the corner shifted. He was holding a Penthouse magazine, but lost interest and tossed it to the floor. His face was thick, and his jowls shook. The part that grabbed my attention was the twelve-gauge pump lying across his lap.

From another part of the house, the sound of a television, a sports game was playing. A chair slid across hardwood floors and then the sound of heavy boots. The door swung open, revealing a man with a stainless steel revolver tucked in the waistband of his trousers. A Ruger Red hawk from the looks of it. His bulk filled the doorway. His blue eyes shined above a radiant smile. His shoulder-length brown hair was curled on the ends. On his right hand, he was nervously playing with a ring wrapped around the middle finger, twirling it around the digit. Every woman probably found him attractive.

He stepped in, closing the door behind him. "Mr. Olsen," he knelt beside the bed, but not too close where I couldn't kick out at him. "I need you to pay attention, you hear me?"

"Fuck off," I croaked. I made it obvious from the start. I wasn't his buddy nor would I ever be.

"Now, George, you're going to listen to what I have to say," he paused, lit up a cigarette. He pulled at his jean jacket, fumbled around inside at the pocket, and pulled out a picture. The picture was of Jill and me. "This is Jill Monroe," he paused, looked at the picture admiringly. "She works at Stubby's Grocery down in Estancia. I have seen her just about every time I've gone there," he looked at the picture. "One fine woman."

I realized I was in trouble, but I couldn't figure out the angles through my roaring hangover. "You don't have the balls," I muttered through gritted teeth.

Erin laughed. "You don't know who you fucking with," he tucked the photo back in his jacket pocket. "Now, I know you came back here for her."

"Are you who I'm supposed to meet?" I croaked.

Erin's sagged, the smile turned into a frown. He looked over to the fat man still seated in the corner. "Well, yes, we are the ones you need to meet," he slapped a hand on my chest. "You know the conditions. In exchange," he held up the picture of Jill. "She gets left alone. I need you to listen carefully. I know it's hard with a fucking hangover."

The man with the shotgun giggled. "Shit, you shoulda seen him drinking! He made an ass outta himself!"

Erin looked back with a mask of annoyance. "Jake, go outside and wait for Bob. I can hear a car coming up the road."

Jake stood up, cradling the shotgun in the crook of his arm. "He's bringing Erika too, right?"

"We already said he was," he shot another look of anger. "She's the other half piece to this puzzle. Now get out there and wait for Bob. Tell him to keep the car running."

Jake wobbled out the door. His face long, drawn like a dog that had been beaten too much, but his eyes held a glint of rage. Still cradling the shotgun, he moved out of the room, his footfalls heavy, faded out through the front door. The fog of the hangover was clearing from my brain.

Erin turned his attention back to me. "Here's the clinch. We leave Jill alone in exchange for your cooperation. You agree?"

I looked away. The ceiling fan spun on. "What do you want with me?"

"The money," Erin's voice whispered.

"Money? I don't know anything about money."

"We have it on good faith you do, something like a cool million," he sucked in the last of the cigarette before dropping it to the floor and mashing it with the heel of his boot. "We also know you're going to want to help us with that aspect of finding said money."

"Someone's fed you some bullshit," I frowned. I realized he was talking about the money Logan and I had found years ago. I wasn't going to let him know that I knew anything. I wasn't even sure how Erin and his boyfriend club were connected in all of this, but I had to play along.

Erin held up the picture of Jill. "I got friends who say different. Last chance, cooperate or no? We fuck up Jill and her life. Help us with the money and you're free. No harm, no foul."

They had me by the balls. I mentally cursed. But something felt off. Something didn't feel right. I wondered if these were who I was supposed to hook up with. I focused on Jill. "You'll leave her alone?"

Erin smiled and held up his hand. "On a stack of Bibles and scouts honor."

I doubted it. I didn't know the end game in this situation. The first chance I got, I was going to bolt, but I had to choose the right time. Right now was not the time. I was going to have to play along for now. "Get me out of these cuffs, and I'll help look."

TWENTY-SIX

"You know," Erika swept her long, dark bangs from her face. "For being friends, you guys are sure are quiet." She was a small package of a woman. Spanish, obviously, but also none too bright it seemed. Maybe I was wrong but she seemed out of the loop on things. Dark eyes, firm legs, firm body, it told me she worked out, trying to stay in shape. She was doing a fine job of it.

"I'm Erika," she held her hand out.

I took it. "George."

"What'd you do?"

"What do I do?"

"For a living?"

I looked to Erin. There was a twinge of jealousy etched on his face. Did Erin have something going with Erika? I wondered. "Diesel mechanic."

"Oh, so are Erin and Bob," she sounded interested.

I didn't give a reply. There wasn't any reason to either. She pulled her hand back. "Everyone is looking for mechanics," she said.

"Erika," Erin muttered.

Erika looked at Erin. "What? We're always looking for mechanics. You complain all the time about how short-handed the shop is."

"Enough, Erika," Erin narrowed his eyes.

Erika looked confused. "What?"

"I don't think George is looking," he looked at me. "Are you, old buddy?"

"No," I answered. "No, I'm not."

The ride had been quiet talking-wise. Judas Priest belted out a song about being a devil's child from the speakers. Barely a word passed between anyone. Bob looked back in the rearview mirror. He was heavy, greasy-looking like he hadn't bathed in a month, and the smell only confirmed it. Once he and Erika pulled into the yard, Erin instructed me to get into the old beat-to-shit four-door Buick. Bob protested but Erin shut him up with a glare. Jake handed Bob my photo of Jill. He told Bob to give them to Erin's friends. That was concerning.

There meant there were more players in the game than what they were telling me. It wasn't unusual for the Cartel to do business with white guys here on this side of the border, but there was something I was missing out of all this. The lingering question was Erin and the Boyfriend Club my actual contacts? I was sure the Cartel were Mexicans.

Bob's eyes filled the rearview mirror. "Smoke? Old buddy?" I asked. I ignored Erika.

Erin fumbled for a cigarette from his shirt pocket, lit one up, and passed it back to me. I kept in mind he still had the Red hawk tucked in his pants.

There were too many people involved, and I didn't know who the other players were. Looking at Erin, he was the ring leader, obviously, but he was being fed a line of shit from someone. Bob...just a follower. His fat face focused on the road in front of us. Looking at Erika, her face pale with uncertainty. I wasn't sure who or why she was here. She might've been Rubin's cousin, but the odds of us meeting like this were astronomical in coincidence. Erin and Bob claimed she was the other half of the puzzle. I wasn't sure what they meant.

That left Jake.

He was following along in the battered old Ford truck but was falling behind. There had been no room in the Buick and he was claiming claustrophobia if he tried. He said he would follow in his truck. I looked back and saw the Ford was struggling to keep up.

"Where we going, old buddy?" I asked.

Erin smiled. "Going to see some friends."

Looking out the side window, I saw we were on some back road outside Estancia. Erin and Bob were taking precautions. If I, or Erika, started anything, we would have hell trying to get to any well-traveled road or even to anyone's house. The land was open fields with the occasional cornrows or pinto bean fields. Plus, it was less likely we would attract any attention from Law Enforcement. Erin's 'old friend' bullshit line had me concerned. Who were his 'friends'?

"What the fuck is Jake doing?" Bob asked.

Erin craned around in his seat, looking between me and Erika with a puzzled look on his face. "Maybe having issues? You know he's had nothing but problems with that shit-box Ford."

"Do we slow down and let him catch up?" Bob asked while swapping looks from the rearview mirror back to Erin.

"Naw, the dumb-shit knows where we're going anyway," Erin

answered.

"Where the fuck are we going?" I asked.

"I'd like to know too, Erin," Erika injected. "Something feels weird about this. Why are we on this road? I thought we were going to the police?"

Erin smiled. "Look, it's a shortcut. We're going to see some friends, pick up a few things, and we're off." He turned and leaned back in his seat. "Everyone relax. It's nothing to worry about."

"I don't know," I said.

"You just be quiet, old buddy," Erin snorted in disgust.

"But I thought..." Erika's voice trailed away to a whisper. Her eyes became filled with confusion. "I thought after...being kidnapped…."

I looked at her in the eyes. She was troubled, her brain trying to figure out what was going on. I didn't say a word but gave a nod in understanding. This was Erika Fernandez. Kidnapped victim missing for the last two weeks. I wondered how she ended up with Erin and his little merry men.

The driver's side window shattered, Bob moaned and there was a thick mist of blood in the air. Erin shrieked like a bitch. I thought for a second he would've blown my head off with the Red hawk, but it fell out of his grasp and tumbled to the floorboard with a loud thud. The Buick swerved, swayed. I seized my chance. Lunging over the seat, I forced Bob's foot down on the accelerator. The Buick roared ahead. I shot a glance over my shoulder. The driver's window spider-webbed, cracked and fell out in pieces. A late seventies Chevy 4x4 truck came roaring up alongside. Behind us, another Chevy except this one looked newer, dark blue. Another spatter of gunfire and metal thumped, paint peeled, flaked, glass shattered.

Erin was screaming while fumbling for the Red hawk. Off to my left was a cornfield. I jerked the wheel hard and went down a ditch and up over into the field. I rose, slammed up against the roof, and fell back over the seat still holding Bob's dead leg hard on the accelerator. Cornstalks folded over, smashing the roof and windshield.

Looking back, Erika was covered in blood, she held out her hands in front of her, a shocked look clouded her face. I had no time to counsel anyone at this point. I made one attempt to lift Bob's dead leg off the pedal, but Erin lunged out, grabbing my arm. The Buick swerved hard to the right. Cornstalks continued beating the windshield to death.

I fought back. A quick elbow shot landed perfectly across the bridge of his nose. He fell back against the car door screaming. A thin ribbon of blood poured through the cracks of his fingers.

The Buick slid and rolled down a ditch. We had cleared the cornfield. I focused my attention on what was ahead. I peered through the only section of the windshield that hadn't splintered or shattered. I moaned through gritted teeth.

Up ahead I saw the dirt berm looming large and fell back. Erin must've seen what was ahead. He lunged out, not to attack but to try and get Bob's leg off the pedal. Seeing it was too late, I dropped back over the seat and braced myself. The Buick rolled up and slammed into the embankment. Judas Priest died mid-scream on the radio.

I heard a scream through the jumbled noise of glass. Dirt and dust exploded inside, obscuring my vision. I slammed forward into the framework of the front seat, my shoulder fell numb. Stars bounced around my vision like Fourth of July fireworks. I groaned through gritted teeth, hissing and cursing. Erika screamed then silence.

Erin rose over the seat, "Jesus..." he exclaimed. His eyes wild with fear. I moaned then rose, then flopped back in the rear seat. There was no need to continue the fight. He knew we were both in the shit. He rubbed the dirt from his eyes. Frantically, he popped the door open, forcing it open on twisted hinges, then staggered out, looking around. He took off into the thick clusters of corn stalks.

I wheezed out a cough of dust. I would've called him a chicken shit for running off, but it was better to save my breath. I had enough sense now. I checked Bob for vitals, but that was a wasted effort.

Bob's face was a jumbled, swollen mess. Covered in dust and dirt, the head wound wasn't bleeding. A bad sign. I pulled the dead weight off the steering wheel. His lifeless eyes were rolled up. He was long gone.

The roar of the Chevy's was inching closer.

I kicked the door open, rolled out, and fell to the ground. I tried catching my breath. My arm was numb from being slammed against the frame in the front seat. I flexed the fingers a few times trying to force the digits to operate. Looking around, I calculated I had but a minute or two before the Mexicans were on top of us.

I started to move away, staggering but halted mid-step. Looking back, Erika was whimpering, shocked at the chaos swirling around us. I had every right to bolt and run and leave her there. I didn't even know if she was Rubin's cousin or not. But there was a damned sliver of humanity that stabbed me right in the chest. I needed answers and Erika might hold them. Erin and Jake had said she was half of the puzzle. Besides, whoever the guys were in the trucks might just end up killing her. She might be an innocent victim.

Staggering back, I dove into the wreckage, grabbed hold of her shoulder, and shook until she was somewhat back to reality. "Erika!" I yelled

She held a shocked, unbelieving expression on her face. She tried to speak but her lips trembled.

"We got to go!" I took hold of her and pulled her out.

"Who…?" The question fell from loose lips.

"I don't know but we got to run. If we can stay hidden in the cornfields and keep moving, we might be able to get back to the highway and flag someone down."

I staggered out, pulling her behind me. Erika looked around in confusion but she was starting to realize we were in trouble. "They're coming closer," she said through quivering lips.

I grabbed her hand and we sprinted, running through the cornrows, disappearing ever deeper within the thick clusters. Erika must've realized just what kind of trouble we were in. She sprinted hard, pushing against the corn stalks pulling ever further ahead of me. If she got too far ahead, we would lose each other.

"Erika!" I yelled. She kept running hard. I yelled again but she wanted away from this mess we were in. She hit an opening where the local farmers had cleared and leveled a section of ground. The two Chevy trucks roared into view. With engines revved on high, Erika stumbled to a stop and tried running in another direction only to get cut off by the second truck.

I stumbled out of the cornfield in time to see the Chevy come roaring up and spun in a circle, kicking up dust and chunks of corn stalks, cutting off any chance of Erika escaping. She stood shaking as the cowboys jumped out and took hold of her and threw her to the ground. The heavier of the two pulled out a large revolver and pressed the barrel to her head. The wall of a man held the pistol steady.

Erika screamed.

I held a hand up as the second cowboy swung the barrel of the M4 up and leveled it off in my direction. Please, oh Father God, let me save one person in all this mess.

"Don't!" I yelled. Stumbling forward, I held my hands out showing I was unarmed.

The Mexican cowboy smiled. A quivering toothpick clenched between his obscenely white teeth. "*Amigo*… hands up!"

The heavy Mexican holding the pistol to Erika's head chuckled. Erika shook in fear.

I realized we were in deep shit.

TWENTY-SEVEN

As I sat in the vast void of darkness, I began contemplating the number of sins I've collected in life. My trust in God had been eradicated while in the Army, for good reason, but did it mean I had to exclude Him from life altogether?

I thought about all the women I had wronged, my failed marriage...the daughter I had seen but a few times over the years. All because I was working on that career as a raging alcoholic and womanizer. The number of times I got tossed into jail for drunk and disorderly.

My daughter...Megan...how old was she now? I thought, calculating the years. She was just shy of nineteen...*Jesus, nineteen.* A shame I only thought of her occasionally, but the bitch mother was the reason. Or was I the true issue in all that? Lord knows I was busy chasing loose women back then. I guess the ex-wife had every right to kick me out of their lives altogether.

Now, here I was wondering how Megan was doing. The mother I could've given two shits about, but my daughter? I wondered what she would think if she ever found out about her old man being tangled up in another fine mess.

"*George!*" Erika whispered. It sounded hollow, echoing in the large room. I figured we were in a large warehouse or barn. I was laying odds on the latter. The faint aroma of horse shit filtered through the thick hood covering my head. "That's your name, right?"

"It is," I said.

Her heavy breathing told me she was on the verge of a major panic attack. "Who are these people?"

"I don't know," I said. "I got enemies all over. Take your pick. Plus your buddy Erin probably turned us over to these clowns, so you can thank him."

"I think they're the same guys who kidnapped me," she whispered.

"You the one in the news then?" I asked.

"Erin and his friends found me and helped get me free," She said.

"But held you prisoner? Didn't you think that a bit odd?"

"Well, no, they wouldn't let me go. They said it was for the best to stick with them in case Diego had friends."

"Diego?" I wracked my brain trying to remember where I'd heard the name 'Diego', and then the newspaper article came to mind.

"Diego Ramirez. I thought he was a friend, but he kidnapped me instead."

"The guy who was found shot out on Highway 41?"

"Yes..." she fell silent.

"Didn't you think that was strange?"

She was silent for a moment. "Not at the time. We were friends."

"Keyword is '*was*', right?" I had to smile under the hood.

"Do you know Erin and his friends?" She asked.

"I was going to ask you the same," I said. "You guys all know each other?"

She was quiet for a minute but figured she didn't have anything else to lose. "We work together."

"Let me guess, the County Line Truck Stop," I muttered.

"How'd you know?"

I shrugged, "Just a wild guess." I knew it had something to do with the money from long ago. It was obvious that Erin and his crew didn't work for the Cartel. They weren't the ones I was supposed to meet up with. Was Erin just some sort of freelancer or was he working for someone else?

My life was shit. First, I'm sold out by someone in the Marshals, then forced to return to this fucking shit-hole by the Cartel, now this mess. I swore. Captured two times in a single day. That had to be a damned record of some sort.

All I wanted was Jill to be safe, find out what the Cartel wanted, which I knew was going to be about the money. My gut told me that. I tell them I knew nothing about it, they agree…hopefully. Then head back to Monahans, maybe with Jill in tow. Then again, she had already moved on in life with another man. What in hell made me think she would even consider that option? I cursed again. Damn, I was stupid.

"George…." Erika whispered.

"What is it?"

"If you escape, take me with you," she said.

"I'll try, okay?" I meant that seriously. With her being kidnapped, then 'rescued' by Erin, then recaptured by the Cartel, she had to know something of value.

We'd had our heads covered up in hoods, bound up, and were thrown into the trucks. From there, I had no idea where we were headed. I had an idea due to the number of times the truck turned or swayed around corners. The telling object was when I heard a train horn blowing off close by and the rattling of steel wheels. Mountainair was the only logical explanation. From that point, the roads felt familiar. The rolling, rising hills, the sounds of cars passing in the opposite direction, the turns. I was sure of it.

Even though my eyes were open, the world was still a black void. My hands were tied behind my back with a set of handcuffs and the legs were bound tight to a metal chair.

I could hear Erika's moans and sniffles of anguish. I wondered if she thought the same things I was. Did she have a kid somewhere? A family that would miss her?

I gave the bindings around my legs and arms a hard flex. After several attempts, there was no way I was going to bust anything or loosen a thread. Whoever had me, wanted me nice and secure.

I groaned and relaxed. I was about to ask Erika if she was Rubin's cousin but then the sound of a door opening made me forget the question. The squealing hinges moaned and a clatter of booted feet filled the void before the door slammed shut. The clicking array of boots on concrete drew closer. I sensed several men gathering around me. The hairs on the back of my neck stood up on end.

The world flashed back into view as the hood was yanked away. I blinked a few times, forcing the eyes to refocus. Erika let out a muffled shriek. I could see she was terrified, eyes filled with tears, mascara running from beautiful brown eyes.

The Mexican with the obscenely white teeth pulled a knife, and slowly cut away the bindings wrapped around my arms and chest. He left the cuffs attached and the ropes around my feet and legs alone. With Erika, it was different. They stuffed a rag in her mouth and wrapped another over her mouth. I felt sorry for her at that moment looking into her terrified eyes.

Eight men stood around us. Eight Mexican cowboys and a couple of gang-banger types. Some held an assortment of ARs, and others had pistols crammed in waistbands. One man was seated across from me, shuffling a deck of cards. He laid them out before him on the table then gently stacked them into a single stack next to another deck of cards.

He raised his head into the light. A flame from a lighter flared to life exposing soft, Spanish features. The zippo slapped shut, extinguishing his face but the orange-tipped glow from the cigarette remained. "You, my friend, how should we say? Are in *mucho la mierda, Comprende?*" He smiled exposing white, perfect teeth.

There wasn't any reason to answer. It was obvious that the situation was precarious.

"*Español?*" He asked

I shook my head. There was no point in telling them anything above what they already knew. I knew a few bits of Spanish here and there. I could speak enough to get me where I needed to go, but I was far from fluent. There was no need for me to tip my hand.

"English it is then," he gave a nod. Three burly Mexicans slung their rifles over their shoulders, took hold of Erika's chair and lifted her, and carried her out of the room. She screamed through the gag, her eyes pleading for me to do something, anything to save her. The door at the end of the barn opened, sunlight spilled in. The trio exited, Erika's muffled screaming came to an abrupt halt mid-scream when the door was slammed shut.

I could see where they were going with this. They wanted to prove they were in control and were using Erika as leverage.

"Spanish is a most civilized language, you should attempt to learn and speak it." He leaned into the outer fringes of the light. "I'm going to ask questions, and you will answer…truthfully." Another drag off the cigarette and a plume of soft smoke filled the silent void between us.

"I don't know who you are," I answered.

He leaned forward, holding his hands out. "I am your savior," he shook his head, leaned back in his chair. "I hope you are not ungrateful for what we have done for you, *amigo.* After we saved you from unsavory men."

"Didn't need any saving," I whispered.

"It is of no concern now. Another drag from the cigarette. We saved you from those bad people, now you owe us, yes?"

The image of Bob's head bursting came into my mind. "I don't know you, and I don't owe you shit."

He snapped his fingers and the Mexican cowboy stepped forward with a bottle of tequila and a shot glass. "My name is Enrique Rivardo, perhaps you have heard of me?" He took the bottle, poured a shot before settling back in the chair. "You have…or will, it is a shame you are so ungrateful. I wish you had performed as instructed and waited in the motel room."

"So you're who I was supposed to meet up with?"

He gave a slow tip of his head. "It is us. You don't believe that you were supposed to be met by those dirty *gringos* we saved you from do you?"

"I didn't know what to think, to be honest."

"Did your mother ever say to never run off with strangers?"

"They had some captivating evidence that said to the contrary," I muttered.

"Did you not know who they were?"

"Not now, I don't."

Enrique leaned back and began laughing. The other men around him also began laughing and giggling. "They were Dixie Mafia, your old friends. See how we saved you?"

I should've seen that coming. Now we got the Dixie Mafia thrown into the mix. My brain could've just melted. I shifted the subject. "Erika?"

He downed the shot. "Safe, but it depends on you for how much longer, *Senor Hendricks*."

I clenched my jaw, working the muscles. "Never heard of him."

He sipped from his glass, dark eyes studying me. He snapped his fingers. Another Mexican stepped forward. He held up a photo. It was several years old, a mirror image of me with longer hair stared back into my eyes.

"Of course you do. You are James Hendricks, a diesel mechanic at Duggan's Truck Stop, just a few years ago. You and a friend of yours, a Logan Pierce, found some money that belonged to us."

I wanted to ask where the hell they got the photo from but held my tongue. I already knew that answer. "You guys making a lot of fuss over half a million."

He mocked surprise. "So, you are Hendricks?"

"Never said I was, but plenty of people around here want to know about this money, of which, I don't know anything."

"Know?"

"About the money," I shrugged.

A man with half his face covered in prison tats stepped out of the shadows and pointed. He wasn't the normal cowboy type. He was pissed off about something. "*No creo una maldita palabra de esta perra!*" He stabbed a finger at me and rattled on. My Spanish was rusty, but I could make out the words '*murder*' and '*shoot this fucker*'. Enrique shook his head and yelled back a retort in rapid, machine-gun Spanish. After several minutes the tatted Mexican stepped back. Enrique clenched his jaw and looked over at me. "Forgive me. Rico believes you are responsible for his brother's death."

"I haven't killed anyone." That was the truth.

"What about a man named Diego?"

"Diego?" I questioned. I knew the answer, but it was best to play stupid.

"He was murdered, in his car a few miles outside of Estancia. A most unfortunate experience. Erika was with him at the time of his demise. Rico holds you responsible."

I remembered the newspaper article. The man shot in his car just outside Estancia. "I remember reading about it, but I didn't know him. That shit happened *before* I got here and he can take that up with Erin and his crew, not me."

The thug with the half-face tattoo leaned over and said something in Spanish. Enrique rattled a response back in an angry tone. They looked at each other for a moment before turning their attention back to me. "Rico says we should just kill you because he believes you are responsible for his brother's death."

"I don't know anything about it," I looked Rico in the eyes. "And Rico here can go fuck himself."

Enrique ignored my comment. "I believe you, Hendricks, but I have other questions for you."

Rico slid back into the shadows, resting a hand on the stainless automatic pistol in the waistband of his trousers.

The silence grew between us. He shifted his weight and leaned across the table. "Some time ago, you and a friend went to look for money buried out somewhere, yes? And you found it."

"No one knows where the money is now."

"You still have not answered my question."

"And I said, yes, we did, but we lost it when the Dixie Mafia came and took it from us."

"I find this hard to believe. You have to know something?"

"Look, all I know is that the money was taken by a group of dirty cops. One of them hid it, An Officer Richardson, and now no one knows where he hid it. Most assuredly, I don't know either."

"But you have dreamed of coming back and finding this money, have you not?"

"No, you could stack that pile and I'd burn it."

"What about Richardson, Officer Richardson?"

"What about him?"

"What do you know of him?"

"Dirty cop, worked for the State Police, he was the one everyone said went and hid the money after they hit the Dixie Mafia and wiped them out."

He smiled, pointed a slender finger toward me. "You will help us recover what is ours."

"I'd rather not."

"This is not an option but an expectation."

"I haven't any idea where the money is or even where to begin looking."

Enrique leaned back in his chair and waved a hand. He took up a card, studied it then reinserted it back into the deck. "Are you familiar with *Braja*?" He continued without explaining. "My grandmother was a *Barja*," he took another card from the deck. "Meaning she was a 'witch' in the *gringos* tongue. She taught me to read fortunes to people. She taught me the cards never lie. Do you believe such things?"

"No."

"We are going to play a game." Enrique continued.

"What're we playing? BlackJack?" I looked around the room. "Naw, how about Old Maid? Seems your guy's style."

No one smiled.

He flipped out two cards from one deck. "King and a joker," he flipped the third card from the other deck, revealing an eye within the moon. "All-knowing."

Another card from the deck was flipped. It looked like an infant riding a white horse under the sun.

"This one means obtaining knowledge, success," Enrique continued.

The last card was turned revealing what looked like a woman spitting into the mouth of a man.

"This one means," he placed a finger on the card. "You will lead us to the fortune," he stabbed a finger on the King card. "The King, means good fortunes for me but the Joker tells me to be wary of you," he shook a finger. "You have a mischievous soul, an untamed spirit, a strong potential to lie for personal gains."

"Look, I don't believe in any of this crap, and another point, which I'm sure I stated before, I don't know anything about where this money is."

"You tell me lies," he rose from his chair, leaned in, and gave a nod. "Luis."

Luis, the Mexican cowboy who had held the M4 on me in the cornfield, grabbed a handful of my hair and pulled back hard. Enrique pulled out a cigarette from a gold case.

"Chavo." The fat man emerged from the shadows. This was the same guy who had put a gun to Erika's head. He was every bit of four-hundred and fifty pounds of fat and muscle, mostly fat. He pulled a knife and held the long, bright blade across my throat. Chavo grunted in amusement. A gold tooth sparkled in the light from the smiling maw.

Enrique smiled. "You do and will," he lit the cigarette. "We will play another card so you understand where you are in the scheme of things." He placed his hand inside his jacket and pulled out another photograph. He smiled and held it up for me to see.

My heart skipped a beat.

Jill smiled from the photograph. Innocent, beautiful, radiant, and unaware of the potential shit-storm swirling around her.

"You know her well, yes?"

"Shit…, I think you already know the answer to that question," I muttered.

"I knew it would be a card you would truly understand," he placed the photograph down on the table in front of me. "You will do as you are told. You will find our money, do you understand?"

"Leave her out of this," I answered.

"We will, I give my word, once we have our money and anything else you find along the way," he turned and walked away. His voice trailed away, but it was easy to understand. "You have but a little time to find our money, *Senor* Hendricks, do you understand?" He nodded. Chavo retracted the knife.

I sat fuming, pissed, realizing there was nothing left I could do. I was trapped in something that was beyond my scope or level of expertise. I also knew one other thing: they weren't going to let me out of this thing alive.

TWENTY-EIGHT

I was dragged out of the trunk of the low rider and dumped out on the dirt ground face first. Chavo had a good chuckle. Luis smirked while handing Rico the key to my cuffs. Rico undid the cuffs while Luis wandered around the outside of the hotel room studying the room number. He took my room key and unlocked the door. He made a few waves to his compadres. The trio of men entered. The sounds of drawers being opened, the bed being tossed came within earshot.

I sat up and rubbed the circulation back in my wrists. I looked around wondering who else was on the campgrounds but there was no one around. Old man Harold was nowhere to be seen. I cringed at the sounds coming from the room. I was afraid they would find the stuff that I had hidden up in the rafters in the bathroom.

After the meeting, Enrique left first through the barn and took off in a Dodge 4x4 with large rims and rubber band tires. Luis and the remaining men bound me up, tossed the black hood over my head, and tossed my ass in the trunk. They had a lot of fun with that. A few hard punches to the kidneys and gut made sure to convey the message they were in charge.

Luis walked out of the motel room, dusting his hands off. The other men trailed out behind him. They had found nothing but the beer in my fridge. Each held a can, cracking them open. "*Amigo*, I like this place. We'll be watching you, understand?" He waved a hand and Rico went to the room next door and popped it open. "Rico and Alejandro will be next door to watch over you. Tomorrow, we start our new adventure to find the pirate's booty." He slapped his hands together, rubbing them furiously in excitement.

I frowned. "You mean the pirate's chest."

Luis frowned in misunderstanding.

"I'm not looking up some dude's ass."

He frowned. "Pirate's chest?"

"Not up his booty."

Luis looked down in careful thought. "I see."

Rico tapped his fingers on the pistol tucked in the waistband of his trousers. Alejandro was a Mexican cowboy. He took out a bag from the back seat of the Buick. I guessed there was an AK or AR stuffed inside.

I staggered up on wobbling feet and brushed the dirt off my trousers. I started to say something but he cut me off with the wave of his hand. "Enrique said it is necessary."

"What about Erika?"

He smiled. "Safe," he tapped the revolver butt with his fingertips and shrugged. "For now."

"That wasn't part of the agreement."

"It is not for me to say," he shrugged.

"She ain't got nothing more to do with this now," I argued.

"Well," he stepped up to within inches of my face. The smell of onions filled the void between us. "It will give you that much more incentive with two lovely women to think of, yes?"

Before I could say anything, he turned quickly, walking back to the small group of friends. They all clamored back in the Buick low-rider. Luis then leaned out of the passenger window holding out a cell phone. "We'll be back but you will start looking for our money first thing in the morning," he lit up a cigarette. "We have eyes everywhere, *amigo.* We will be watching…" he paused, lit up a cigarette. "We will assume you have gone to the police and your women will suffer for it, *comprende?*"

"Yeah," was all the strength I could muster for an answer.

In a cloud of dust, the low-rider spun off. I stood there in the dusty mist under the yellowing skies of dusk. I gritted my teeth. First Erika, now Jill. I really could care less about Erika but she was now an unwilling pawn being used to leverage my cooperation in finding the missing money. I didn't feel like having her getting killed on my account though. My conscience could barely stand the thought that Jill was involved.

I turned. Rico stood near the door next to my room. He smiled, nodded, and waving a hand. I walked past him. I caught a glimpse inside their room. Alejandro was loading a magazine into an AK-47. I stepped into my room, closing the door behind me. Rico waved and had a smile showing off several gold teeth. Now there were additional problems. I was sure Rico would rather put a bullet in my hide than deal with watching over me. Two guards, no viable way to escape, but I'd come up with a plan.

But there was a whisper of hope, a small glimmer of salvaging something from this mess. I dug around in my back pocket and found the wadded-up chunk of paper. Luis and the gang had stopped to grab a bite to eat just a short time after cramming my ass in the trunk. While they ate, they tossed the wrappers in the back.

I slowly undid the crumpled waxy paper and read the letters stamped across the grease-stains. I knew the restaurant well enough. I had eaten there a time or two a few years ago. I knew the place had been in business for the better part of fifty years.

El Antojitos.

I mulled over the locations of the restaurant. It had been a while but I knew for certain there were only two. One being in Albuquerque up on the west side and the other was just south of Belen off Highway 47. Albuquerque would've been too far, The Belen location though was just about right travel time-wise.

On the next note, I kept a mental count from the time the low rider pulled out of Enrique's compound. I counted the seconds off until we hit the hardtop and recounted from that point up until they stopped at El *Antojitos.*

The room had been ransacked. The blank notepad and pen had been swept to the floor. Picking up both items, I scribbled the numbers down.

Eight hundred and seventy-five seconds on the dirt road and two cattle guards, then another two thousand three hundred and eighteen second-count on the asphalt.

It wasn't perfect, but at least I had an idea where Enrique's hideout might be situated. I also knew I was going to have to figure out how to get Erika out of this mess.

But the options were getting limited.

TWENTY-NINE

I opened the fridge. There were several cans of Old Milwaukee left. At least they hadn't grabbed all of them. I took a can, cracked it open, and drained it in several large gulps. I took another can from the fridge and surveyed the damage. They had tossed the room pretty well. I went into the bathroom, stood on the toilet, and pushed the vent cover to the side. I felt the medical kit and the Browning pistol and felt a sigh of relief. It was tempting to take the Browning and go blast Rico and Alejandro in the face, but that would raise all kinds of alarms. Marge and Harold would damn near have a heart attack if a gun battle broke out on their property. Then, escaping from the cops would just complicate matters. I pushed the Browning aside and took down my computer before sliding the panel back in place.

I spent an hour cleaning up. The ransacked room looked

better than when I first arrived in my opinion. The day had slowly eroded to the dark tones of dusk.

Satisfied they hadn't found anything other than my beer, I went to the kitchenette. After several minutes, the coffee pot began gurgling the black liquid gold.

I spent most of the remaining day thinking and dragging up the old files on the laptop. Thinking can be a bad thing, but it was all I had. I fired off the 'net and began scouring for anything of value. Within an hour I figured someone had sold out everyone from Erin's little gang.

Bob was dead, which ruled him out permanently as a suspect. Erin ran off to God-only-knew-where. If he knew anything, he was laying low at the moment. If they were connected to the Dixie Mafia as Enrique had said, then the Dixie Mafia already knew what had happened. Erika wasn't ruled out of the equation either. She could be playing along as an innocent victim but was working for Enrique. And then there was the last man in the whole gang that no one knew if he had lived or died.

Jake.

He was supposed to be following us but somewhere along the way, he fell off. No one within Enrique's gang had mentioned anything about him but then again, they hadn't spoken about Bob or Erin either.

The two main suspects. Erin and Jake. I was guessing Erin was with Jake, both hiding somewhere. I just wasn't sure where or why. I replayed the images in my mind, trying to capture key moments. Erin looked too damned scared like he didn't know what the hell was going on or who was attacking us. I still couldn't rule him out.

I tapped away on the computer. The next search was about the circumstances with Logan. There wasn't much out there in the land of ether but a few scraps of information. I was able to string together a fragmented picture of what had happened. I hit on a series of articles about the death of five Dixie Mafia members and the sordid details with the five New Mexico State cops involved in the shootout.

Richardson, the main ring leader involved, had blown his brains out with his service pistol when the FBI came knocking. The interesting thing was the article mentioned he was from Mountainair and was stationed there. I looked up other articles related to the trials of the other men involved. Two others were also stationed with Richardson. Their domain encompassed the whole of Torrance County and all five officers lived or had family roots within the community.

Richardson had been married but according to the article, he also had a side bitch by the name of Mary Higgins. She was a two-bit stripper who had worked at the 203 strip joint just outside Moriarty. She didn't know anything about any money.

A connection?

I hadn't known about the 203 connection. Did Mary Higgins still work there? Had she been the one to put the finger on me? I found a mugshot of her and tried looking it up on any of the typical social media pages but came up with a zero. The final bit of info I could find on her was that she had moved away from Torrance County not too long after the debacle. I ruled her out as being involved.

I went back to the article. Higgins testified she had seen Richardson pack two large duffel bags in the trunk of his squad car and rolled out south on 41. She knew they were packed down with cash because Richardson had opened one of them and handed her a stack of fifties amounting to around five grand.

I studied the wall and cracked open my second beer. I had done well to curb my liquor intake. Well, except for last night. Usually, by now I would've finished off a six-pack. I mulled over past events. When Logan and I had found the money it was stuffed into nine ammo cans, not two large duffel bags. Somewhere along the way, Richardson and his squad had picked up a fair amount more money.

It led back to the shootout. I searched for any articles about the incident. None of the articles mentioned anything about large bags of money, except for one. A reporter from the Santa Fe Times wrote about the courtroom drama. The article talked about money being stuffed in large bags. The way it was written, made it all sound like a footnote. No one knew the amount, but the reporter made it sound like thousands.

I was thinking millions.

The difficulty was figuring out where Richardson went that night. I knew he had some property in Mountainair with his wife, but beyond that, I didn't know anything else. I continued reading the articles and pieced together that after he left Mary Higgins's place.

I bought up the Torrance county map and studied it for a while.

From where Mary Higgins lived in McIntosh to his wife's house in Mountainair, it was about thirty to forty-five minutes away. But there was a four to five-hour window. His wife distinctly remembered him removing his duty gear from the trunk. She also mentioned there were no duffel bags present. He had dumped the money somewhere along the way.

According to my math, figure an hour out and an hour back drive time-wise. That left a couple of hours to stash the duffel bags. He buried it somewhere, but the question was where?

Another search and I came up with Richardson's obituary. It was short and to the point. There was no glorious fanfare, no mention of his service as a State Police officer, nothing. His obituary did mention that his family roots were from Claunch and Pinos Wells.

I bought up the map again and studied it. Claunch was about thirty miles south of Mountainair. A small spec on the map. Probably still inhabited by families who hadn't realized the place was borderline ghost town material. Pinos Wells, on the other hand, didn't show on the map. I did a separate search and found it was a genuine ghost town out in the desolate eastern part of Torrance County. The few photos on the internet showed a fancy Catholic church and a well-maintained cemetery. The rest of the town was nothing more than crumbling adobe relics dating back to the late 1800s. The only claim to fame was that it was the site of New Mexico's first political assassination.

Pinos Wells…

I studied the map, trying to visualize a pattern. I saw it was near Dave Musgrave's old ranch just off Highway 42. It was approximately a fair forty miles give or take. Connection? It didn't make any sense for Richardson to drive to Pinos Wells.

Doing the math, it looked like Claunch was the better option. The four or five-hour missing time gap could easily be explained if Richardson went there. Rereading the obituary made no mentioning of other towns. It was a sure bet that the Feds had scoured these areas with a fine-toothed comb.

On the off chance, I searched for Chavez family roots in Claunch. There were multiple hits and a golden nugget was thrown in my lap. Several photographs had been posted by family members on several genealogy sites. One photo stuck out. It was a photograph of a house with several Chavez family members out in front. I took my cell phone and snapped a picture.

My mind focused back on the missing money.

In reality, the half-million in cash the media was talking about was a trivial amount. Why would anyone think that the money was worth dying for? The present body count was standing at an even two people…three if you counted Rico's brother who was shot on Highway 41 just outside Estancia. But that occurred before I got here. Who else was in this equation? I knew I had to be leaving out somebody.

Then the Dixie Mafia. The Mafia was a large network of mostly family-oriented criminals. I wasn't sure who they all were, but I was sure they had a family connection to Thomas Hauser and his cousins, Robert Lee and Cleeve. Whoever they were, they were nowhere to be seen.

Why did Enrique want to get to the money?

When Logan and I had originally found the quarter mill, there was a large cache of military-grade weapons. All were US military-connected, stolen from various military installations across the southwest. It wouldn't be far-fetched to assume that, besides the money, there were additional guns, or possibly drugs to be found with the missing money. These Cartel boys weren't just after money. Why else take a chance raising hell on this side of the border?

I banged away on the keyboard, typing in court records searching at the Federal and State levels. I had to pay for the court documents in advance. I continued searching the duffel bag angle. After several minutes of searching, I found what I was looking for.

I finished reading the report. Logan had stated in court, there were two large duffel bags stuffed with money. If there were two duffel bags of cash floating around, it wasn't a measly half a million. I was calculating a minimum of five million.

Jesus…five million, maybe more. That amount alone would set anyone up for life.

But there had to be more to it.

Guns?

The news channels across the country were reporting about some operation the Feds were running, something about '*Fast and Furious*'. The operation had turned sour somewhere along the line, and people were dying on both sides of the border. There had to be guns, money, and possibly drugs.

The latter scared the shit out of me. Drugs could get anyone killed. It gave reason to understand why Enrique and his gang were looking for the money. With the money, everything else would be found. What they hadn't figured on was that Richardson was one step ahead of everyone. Even from beyond the grave he was toying with everyone, elusive.

I looked up from the computer screen, rubbed my eyes, and lit up a cigarette. Stepping outside, the setting sun was a blood orange orb that was setting on the horizon. Alejandro sat on a bench that was placed by their room door. He gave a small smile. I smiled in return. The game I was playing involved too many people.

And who was going to die when this was all said and done?

THIRTY

I walked to the 203 strip club just as the sun hovered above the morning horizon. I carried the medic bag under my arm. Since I was heading out to explore an unknown area of remote land, it was better to have it and not need it. The Chevy was still parked in the same spot where I'd left it. I was thankful for that. I didn't feel like explaining to Harold I'd lost his truck.

Getting away from Rico and Alejandro was easy enough. Rico was propped up against the wall dozing outside the motel room door. The sounds of Alejandro snoring in the next room vibrated through the walls. I went out the bathroom window. Before leaving, I scribbled a note to Rico and the gang and left it on the pillow. If my hunch was correct, I'd have a bit of leverage to play with. It was a long shot if I was right or not.

I jumped in the Chevy, fired it off, and hauled ass down Martinez Road then hooked a left on Highway 41. Within thirty minutes, I cruised through Estancia, ignoring Stubby's Grocery store, and turned on 84 toward Mountainair. At the four-way stop, I proceeded south on 54. Along the way, I thought up my plans of action for the day when the cell phone rang.

I grabbed and flipped it open. A husky voice began speaking. "Where are you, *amigo*?"

"Up and moving."

"That is not what I asked. Where are you now? And how did you get a vehicle?"

"Looking and I borrowed a vehicle," I left out what I was driving or who I borrowed it from.

"Where? You were not to leave the motel, *amigo*."

"Talk to Rico and his boyfriend. I left them a note." I tossed the cigarette out the window. "You did get the note?"

"That is not the point. You were not to leave," he paused long enough to let off a string of obscenities in machine-gun Spanish. "You forget your women!"

"Hold up now. I'm getting you the information. That's what you wanted. I'm going to get it. That was our agreement."

"How so? A good reason, *amigo*!"

"Going to Estancia, check out some court records." I was gambling with that statement. I was hoping his gang wouldn't dare show up at the courthouse. The police station was in the same building.

There was a long pause. "Why you go there?"

"Research records to Richardson's estates, property, his Last Will kind of thing," I lied. "I thought you would be ecstatic about that. I get you the information and we can move on to the next step."

Another pause. "Keep us posted. We will meet you in

Mountainair, at the High Desert Cafe," he sounded disgusted. "Noontime. If you're not there, we will assume the worst."

"Right," I pressed end and flipped the phone shut. I could imagine the hell Rico was receiving about now. It didn't hurt my feelings any either.

Claunch. Richardson's family roots extended there. Once things bottomed out at Pinos Wells, the Chaves clan migrated to Claunch in hopes of a better future and better farming. They did well for a time until the Dust Bowl drought hit in the 1930s but they stuck it out and made a small fortune selling their pinto beans to the US Government during World War Two. After the war, things died off for the town and the family. A drought in the 1950s sealed the deal. With no demand for their beans, the drought, the Chaves clan packed it in and moved to Mountainair to live out the rest of their lives.

Richardson's grandparents passed away in the 1970s and were buried on their old lands in Pinos Wells. The lands in Claunch and Pinos Wells were then passed down to his father who passed away in the 1980s. Since Richardson was the only child in the clan, the lands were passed down to him.

It made sense to me that somewhere on either land lay the money and whatever else the Cartel was looking for. My money was on Claunch. It was close enough to Mountainair, right by Richardson's ranch south of town. I imagined he wanted to keep it close but not too close in case it was ever found by accident. He would have no connection to it.

If I found the money, which statistically equated to finding a hundred virgins packed in a single whorehouse, I'd have a bit of leverage. I planned to take a few pictures with the cell phone camera, message those over to Luis, then negotiate for Jill, Erika, and me. A simple plan, but there were too many cracks to fill. The main bone of contention was that the Cartel couldn't be trusted. They were holding all the cards.

The single card I had but was unsure about was contacting the Marshals. I sure as hell didn't trust Lane. I'd opt for another agent, or maybe obtain an attorney. A sure bet, I was looking at prison time this go around, but there was a single thread of hope. I was sure someone within the Marshal's ranks had passed off information to the Cartel. That information alone might spare me the joy of sucking down rotten jail-house hooch while serving a twenty-year stretch.

I rolled up to the town limits of Claunch and pulled over on the shoulder. I pulled out the map and GPS locations. After studying the map for a few minutes, I rolled back on the battered blacktop and rolled through Claunch for about five miles before I found what I was looking for. There were no roads leading to the old house. The ones that had been there were long overgrown. The Chevy sputtered. It had developed a small misfire that seemed to get worse with each press on the accelerator.

The Chavez house was a lone skeleton of dried, grayed, and black wooden planks. The structure leaned. Its front door missing and the broken windows resembled black holes that led to another dimension. It looked like a leering, sun-bleached corpse rotting away under the New Mexico seasons. Off to the far end of the land, impressions from old pinto bean fields could be seen. The small, long, sloped mounds had long since overgrown with dead, dried prairie grass.

I held up the phone, studying the picture of the old Chavez house. I looked up through the windshield. The house was near identical. The overgrown path to the old house was the only way in. The only barrier was a single gate made of rusted pipe that hadn't been opened in years, maybe decades. I killed the ignition on the truck and stepped out. I clambered over the pipe fence, hoping the rusted metal was strong enough to hold my weight.

I took out the paper and made sure the coordinates matched with what was read out on the GPS Garmin device. I walked closer to the house cramming the folded paper in my back pocket. The golden prairie grass rustled and rippled in the light breeze. It was evident no one had been out here for years, but under it all, it was also the perfect disguise.

Various pieces of rusted old farm equipment lay rotting away about the property. Walking around the border of the house, I came across the only bit of modern luxury and proof that the old Chavez place had been visited sometime in recent years. A ladder. An Aluminum ladder with a heavy growth of weeds trying to devour it.

I took a step closer, knelt, and felt the cold aluminum under my fingertips. I glanced up. The roof was a rotting mess and hadn't seen maintenance in decades.

Taking the pin light out of my pocket, I thumbed it on and poked the weak beam inside. My eyes followed the beam through the rotten, dried slats and I saw nothing unusual. There were a few pieces of broken furniture, an old rock fireplace, and a ton of debris that had fallen over the years strewn about the floors.

The back door beckoned me to enter. I wasn't sure if the floor was strong enough and tested it with the weight of one foot first, pressing down on the rotten boards. I entered cautiously, moving forward, shining the light around and in front of me. The light caught something on the floor. I stopped and looked down through the hole in the floor. There was a cellar of some kind under the floor. The dirt floor below was an easy ten feet down.

Which meant there was a way down?

I found it in what used to be the kitchen. Off to the side by another doorway that led outside. I knelt, pulling away the few boards to expose the doorway that led down under the house. It took a few minutes to dig out the dirt from around the latching mechanism before twisting it open. A dark maw opened up. The flashlight exposed no ladder or stairs leading down.

I exited the house, checked the Chevy by the road, making sure no one was bothering with it. Not a soul had driven past since I parked there. Tugging the ladder free from the weeds, I entered the house again, wary that the floorboards might give way under my weight. I shoved the ladder down the trapdoor. I took a deep breath and the first step down.

Dust filaments floated in the air. Cobwebs hung silently from all corners. I was aware there might be Black Widows or even nests of Brown Recluse spiders nestled within them. After wiping away the worst of the webs, I clambered down, hit the floor. There was sunlight drifting down from above. The gentle rays spilled through the cracks between the boards. Where the sunlight failed to illuminate, the penlight filled in the dark voids.

There was one area, just in front of me that held my interest. The walls were lined with rough, uneven boards. I held my light on a section that appeared to have been cut, removed, and patched. Small puffs of dust kicked up with each step forward, I stifled a sneeze. I knelt in front of the wooden wall and inspected the seams. I tapped on it. The section was hollow sounding.

No way could it be this easy.

Modern screws were embedded deep within the wooden planks. Climbing out of the trapdoor, I went back out to the truck, grabbed a screwdriver, and returned to work the screws buried in the wood planks. I wiped away the sweat that began dripping into my eyes. Carefully backing off the screws until they were loose enough to be removed by hand. I worked the plank out of place and poked the light into the dark.

I was close, so close but in the end, there was nothing there. Inside was a hole that had been carved out of the dirt and then encased in planks of wood. The thing that stuck out was that the wood was pressure-treated and still had that greenish hue in some spots. Richardson, or somebody, had used this spot at one time to hide his shit but had moved it to another location or came to cash it out.

I stood up. Anger raced through my veins.

"*FUCK*!" I kicked the ground.

I was sure Richardson was laughing from beyond the grave, but it was just the wind blowing through the rotten wooden slats.

THIRTY-ONE

I was hoping for easy, but things had turned sour. I was running out of options and possible locations. I spent half the morning scouring the house with no results. I searched the barn for anything that indicated Richardson had been there, but again, I came away empty-handed. The only evidence that he had been anywhere out here was the ladder and the large cubby hole down in the house basement. All roads led to the fact he had been out here.

Before leaving, I placed the plank back in its place and tossed the ladder back outside where I had found it. There was still the possibility that the son of a bitch had it stashed out here, but there were no signs of a path anywhere. Even after a couple of years of non-use, there would be some indications of a path, a walkway, a place where a vehicle had been riding over the land, but there was nothing.

For the moment, the old Chavez place held dear to its secrets.

I stood under the sun, sweaty, dirty, and thirsty. I wiped away the sweat, shook my head. Wandering back to the Chevy, my thoughts were blank. After a few cranks, it fired off. The sound of the power steering let off a high-pitched squeal when I turned the wheel hard in performing a U-turn. I drove through Claunch and toward Mountainair.

On the drive back to Mountainair, the radio played the game. Detroit was barely hanging on in their lead over Kansas City. Any other time in history, I would've been kicking back somewhere in the oilfields listening to ball games on the radio or, if time permitted, watching on the TV.

All I could think about was the empty stash hole in the cellar lamenting the fact that nothing was in there. A barrage of questions rained across my mind. Had someone else, by some weird off-chance, found the money? Had Richardson moved what was in the hole to another location? Or, the worst thought yet, what if nothing had been there at all?

I gave up thinking about any of it. I found myself in Mountainair. I spotted the cafe on the corner and rolled into a parking spot. I went in and found a booth. There were several patrons, all busy stuffing their maws. A waitress plopped a menu down on the table and took off. I studied the menu in silence.

A pair of shadows loomed over the booth. Luis slid in next to me while Chavo sat across from us.

"Progress?" Luis asked. "And you better have something."

"So nice of you to just stop in."

Luis looked around. "You didn't answer the question."

I looked back down at the menu. "Nothing."

He smiled. "You are trying my patience."

I laid the menu down. "And I'm trying."

"What do you have?"

"An old ranch house that belonged to Richardson," I deliberately omitted the name of the town.

The waitress returned. Only Chavo placed an order. Chile cheese fries. I ordered a coffee. Once the waitress left. The questions resumed.

"Nothing else?"

"There wasn't much on records. Richardson left some property to his wife is about all I found."

"We know this already, Claunch?"

I leaned back in the booth wishing I had the 9mm on me. "Look, what more do you want? You think I can pull the money out of my ass?"

"That's a stupid thing to say."

"But it was worth looking into, right?"

The bantering questions continued for several minutes until he recognized the fact that he wasn't getting any more information than he already knew. You could see the thoughts racing across his eyes as they darted back and forth. The waitress returned with Chavo's order of fries. He quickly dug into them.

"We will help you."

"I don't need any help," I countered.

He shook a finger and nodded his head. "This is not debatable. How can we trust you when you ran away this morning?"

Chavo jammed a finger load of chili fries into his maw, then sucking his fingers clean, he grunted in satisfaction before blowing wind, attracting the attention of several nearby patrons.

"*Di perdoneme, maricon*," Luis whispered harshly.

"*Lo siento, mi estomago esta gaseoso*," Chavo replied.

"Didn't you bring medicine?"

Chavo winced. "*Dormitorio…El Armidillo.*"

Luis took his hat off and began fanning the air in a weak attempt to wave away the sewer-like stench. "He has a gassy stomach, perhaps we will pick up something for him on the way back to your place."

"Wait, what?"

Luis smiled. "Ah! I knew you would be surprised. We will be staying with you, *amigo*."

THIRTY-TWO

It was near six in the morning when I gave up trying to sleep. With Chavo's incessant grunting and farting, I couldn't handle much more of the sounds nor the rotten noxious fumes that now permeated the stale air within the confines of the motel room. Even the AC unit was of little use. Cracking open the window gave only mild reprieve.

I slid my boots on. I lifted my head above the foot of the bed. Chavo lay sprawled out on the bed, his massive belly rolled over the edge damn near touching the ground. Beside him lay Luis. His hand rested on the handle of a Ruger Red hawk tucked into the waistband of his trousers. It would be wishful thinking on grabbing those hand-cannons without raising too much hell in the small confines of the room. It was a safe bet that Chavo had a pistol hidden somewhere within the rolls of fat. I lamented the fact that there was no way I could get my 9mm from the bathroom rafters.

I crawled to the door, twisted the handle, tugged, and slipped outside. I took a deep thankful breath of fresh air. I had to do something and it would have to happen today. My mind was drawing a blank. I didn't have a gun, a knife, anything. Going against two Cartel thugs barehanded was out of the question also. I could hold my own in a brawl if it came down to it, but having to handle a hulking man like Chavo presented too many problems. A man had to recognize his limitations.

We had spent the night going over the details. Luis demanded that we go out to the ranch in Claunch. I nixed the idea. I opted for Richardson's old house back in Mountainair. Luis didn't like the idea that Richardson's wife might still be living there or the prospect of nosy neighbors. We argued back and forth. Chavo watched the argument with mild amusement. After a while, he flipped on the TV and found a local Spanish station. Luis went outside and made a phone call. I was assuming it was to Enrique. Once back in the room, his whole attitude changed. He was too damn nice. He told me flat-out, we were going to Claunch in the morning. That was the end of the discussion.

That had me curious. It also made me leery.

A gentle breeze kicked up under the morning skies of painted blue and watermelon streaks. The flare of the lighter singed the hairs of a two-week growth just under my nose. The cigarette bloomed to life and I inhaled the gray smoke. The acrid fumes did little to cover up the septic tank stench that clogged my nostrils.

The morning sun had just begun to peek over the horizon, chasing away the remnants of the nighttime shadows. Thoughts swirled in my brain, wondering about the next move. Running was out of the question. There was nowhere to go. The Cartel had people all over. I sure didn't like the idea of living with one eye always looking over my shoulder. My option was to ride out the storm but puzzles of the bigger picture were still forming. In all of it, I was nowhere closer to anything.

But…

Erika…

How did she fit into all this?

Why was Enrique holding onto her? That was a question that needed to be explored. There was no solid reason for him to hold onto her unless...there was a reason. The rat bastard already had my balls in a twist with the threat looming over Jill. That was the real reason I was sticking around, but Erika?

I was drawing a blank.

Wait…

I started to flick the butt away but the name began materializing within the fog of memory.

Fernandez...

Erika Fernandez. Jesus...possible relations with Arturo Fernandez? The state cop indicted on murder, racketeering, and God only knew what else? Arturo Fernandez was close to Richardson and his murdering crew of State cops.

Which meant...

I looked at the motel room door. Chavo and Luis still slumbered within. I frowned in anger. I hadn't seen it up until now. They didn't need me anymore. Somehow, Enrique had figured out a piece of the puzzle. He might even have figured out where the money was located. The realization slowly emerged. The more I thought about it, the angrier I got. Erika knew something I didn't but Enrique did. She either knew something or perhaps had something physically. Chavo and Luis were only here for one thing: to kill me off...today. Why else would he be so damned determined to go out to Richardson's old family ranch?

It was perfect. We all head out to the ranch. It would be secluded and easy to bump me off with a quick shot to the head. My corpse wouldn't be found for years, maybe decades.

They wouldn't hesitate to kill Jill either. I was sure there were plans to make my murder and hers, look something like a murder-suicide. Erika was the main element. I needed her alive to tell me what she knew. She had to know where Jake was hiding or at the least, where he lived. Erika was the ever-evolving piece to the puzzle. The only thing about the angle in this mess was what was Jake's ultimate role in all of this if any at all? I couldn't rule out he and Erika were somehow in this together. I felt determined to find the truth. Erika was probably hoping and praying that I, or anyone, would come to her rescue. The sad element was Jill was oblivious to all of it. She might've sold me out to the Marshals before, but she didn't deserve a death sentence.

I needed a gun, a weapon, or something.

I walked over to the Chevy and rummaged through it. Seeing nothing, I slammed the seatback in place. I finished the cigarette and tossed the butt, my mind still drawing on a blank until…

The rolled-up medic pack lying on the floorboard. The rusty gears of a plan began to grind away the desperation. Opening the pack, I rummaged through the narcotics vials with quick, trembling fingers. The morphine injectors might have value but in the long run, would provide no immediate effect. Narcan would just make them drowsy and besides, there was only a single injector. I needed something enough for both of them. Rummaging further, I found a single five-milliliter vial of Fentanyl.

There were a half dozen syringes and enough Fentanyl to kill both of them. Chavo might need a bigger dosage though given his size. Looking up to the sun, I winced. It was worth a gamble with a single dose and how to administer it? Sure, with a syringe but how to inject them individually and without alerting the other?

Tearing open the package containing the syringe, I plunged the needle into the vial and pulled the plunger back sucking in half the vial. Tearing open the second package, I emptied the vial. I balled up the packages and empty vial and tossed them behind the seat. Having both syringes loaded, I had to think about the next step: how to get them into the ass of Chavo and Luis.

I wrapped each syringe in between a couple of large gauze packs. I lifted my foot, pulled the jeans up over my boot, and slid the gauze pack inside. I tugged the jeans down over the top. Wincing, I had to be careful. One prick of the needle and I was done for. At least in the boot, it would be easy to open and grab the syringes.

I rolled up the medic kit, tied the clasps back together, and tossed it behind the seat.

"*Amigo*," the voice made me spin in place. Luis crouched back, making it like he was going for the Red hawk tucked in his trousers. He laughed instead. "I had you!"

"That you did," I said without a smile.

"What are you doing?" He asked.

I took the map off the dashboard. "I think we do need to go out to Richardson's grandparents' house, just like you said."

"Huh?" he grunted with concerned eyebrows. "I thought you were against this?"

"I was, but," I unfolded the map and stabbed a finger on the map. "There is a spot, a low dent in the ground. There's a path running to it. A cellar, I think."

Luis looked at the map, but his eyes wandered over the interior of the truck. Finding nothing suspicious, he cautiously looked at the map. "Of course, we go look. I am glad you are starting to see things our way, *amigo*."

Chavo exited the room. With a great yawn, he stretched out

and mumbled something about being hungry. A chrome-plated Star Model B 9mm pistol glared under the sun's rays. It was tucked within his great rolls of belly fat.

Luis looked at me with a curious eye. "We will, but first we eat."

THIRTY-THREE

Chavo's stomach grumbled. He started complaining he was still hungry. Luis frowned and shrugged his shoulders. The two were arguing about when to eat and when to work. The conversation was all in Spanish but I was stitching together what was being said. Enrique had instructed them to finish the job...today. Luis didn't specify any further. Chavo waved a hand. He said he would handle it but insisted Luis go get food. It would be finished by the time he returned.

I was pretending to be studying the doorway to the Chaves house. It was going to end here one way or another. We had hit the Lottaburger in Moriarty and grabbed a few burritos to go before hauling ass to Claunch. A syringe full of Fentanyl in a burrito would've been perfect but the timing was in no way in the cards. I volunteered to go in and pay for them but Luis insisted Chavo do it. I started to suspect Luis was thinking I was up to no good.

The gears in my mind were whirling like a well-oiled machine, almost too anxious. I had to constantly remind myself to relax. Eyeing Luis, I wanted that guy dead. He was a direct threat to Jill, Erika, and me.

"Chavo is hungry," he rubbed his nose. I'll go to that little cafe in town."

I came out of the house. "Grab me a drink."

He was silent and then. "Sure...*amigo.* What kind?"

"A coke would be fine."

Luis smiled. "So everyone wants a coke. So three Cokes?" He spun away, walking back to the Buick. He gave Chavo a verbal warning. His face frowning. Chavo grinned, waved a hand, and repeated he would handle it.

The Buick bounced away back through the gate and made a left. I went back into the house. Chavo followed. The floorboards under him groaned in protest. We found the cellar door and I faked understanding what it was. Chavo and I stood facing one another. His face blank, emotionless. "You find," he pointed down the cellar entrance.

"Find?"

"*Dinero,*" he pointed again.

"*Dinero?*" I faked understanding.

"Money*? No español?*"

"No."

Chavo grunted. "Go down." He pointed down the hole.

I was hesitant but he hadn't pulled his pistol. Was he waiting for me to get half-way down the ladder before blasting? I took hold of the ladder, keeping an eye on Chavo. At any moment he was going to do something but he didn't. He watched me move down the ladder and I touched the ground. Looking up, he stood there, like a mountain. I could tell he was mentally calculating when to strike. He was quiet, more than usual, his face blank, nothing like his usual neutral or happy self.

I backed away. I maybe had a few minutes before it all started. I stumbled over some debris, turned, and stepped over another pile of debris. I reached over and tossed some boards around, more to make noise that I was working as directed. I broke a few boards, grunting just enough to give the illusion I was doing something. Chavo's shadow loomed over the entranceway. After a few minutes, I paused. I stayed quiet for a long minute.

"What's going on?" Chavo bellowed.

Here goes, I thought.

"Jesus!" I yelled up the ladder.

"What?" Chavo grunted

"I found it!" I yelled in jubilation.

"Bring it up," he waved a massive paw.

"I can't, it's too much!"

He looked down with a curious expression. His hand on the 9mm. "Like, how much?"

"The wall is full of it. There's no way I can move it all by myself and I need help removing the wood planks covering it all."

He scrunched up his face, his bald head rippled. "*Mucho*?"

"C'mon! I need a hand." I moved away out of view. I reached down, struggling with my trouser leg.

He was either stupid or he was hoping there was money down here. At least he would have something to show Luis. He mumbled something about losing weight when he settled his massive foot on the first rung. The ladder creaked under his weight. I hoped to hell it'd hold. He touched the ground. His feet were planted firmly on the ground. "Where?"

"Over yon, "I said. I started to think maybe he wasn't too

bright after all.

He stumbled forward, stepping on or over the rotten boards and assorted debris. "I see nothing."

I fumbled with my trouser, struggling to pull up the leg over the boot. "It's right there."

"I don't see anything."

I pulled the gauze pack out, fumbling for one of the syringes. "You don't see all that?"

"No."

Lunging forward, I held the syringe low. I had to hit an artery or vein and quick. Being damn fat as he was, that was hard to determine in the dark. I couldn't chance in hitting any fatty tissue. He'd still die but it would be long after he'd wrung my neck. The base of the skull would be the best choice.

He spun. His eyes went wide when he saw the syringe in my hand. With a quick backhanded swipe, his massive paw struck me across the jaw. The blow sent me flying back, tumbling over the clutter of boards. He fumbled for the 9mm but it snagged on the folds of his belly.

My free hand searched the floor. I kept the syringe close in the other. My fingertips found a small section a board. I grabbed it and I jumped back on my feet. I had never thrown anything in my life with any measure of accuracy, but I think even the best baseball pitchers would've been proud. I threw it with such force it shattered across Chavo's face. The 9mm tumbled from his fingers and plopped to the dusty ground just in front of him. I charged forward with everything I had, slamming into his midsection. All, I managed to do was push him back a few inches. He grunted in amusement.

He slammed a paw down on my back. I screamed, collapsed. He grabbed ahold of the back of my shirt and threw me against the wall. Stars bounced around my vision. I started kicking out with a booted foot.

If this continued any longer, I wouldn't have enough energy left. I gasped, coughed. He kicked me several times to the midsection, knocking the wind out of me. If I didn't get a move on, he was going to kill me with his bare hands.

The moment wasn't too long in waiting.

Chavo reached down, grabbed me with both arms, engulfing me in a massive bear-hug. I reared back screaming as the bones in my back popped. I clutched the syringe in one hand. Through the grace of God, the one arm that held onto the syringe was free. My other arm firmly clamped in Chavo's death grip. I let off a scream and in one swift motion, stabbed the syringe right into his left eye, slamming the plunger home.

Chavo's eyes went wide. His breath ceased and then with a gasp, his bear hug relaxed. I slipped out and fell to the floor in a heap, gasping.

He fanned his arms, staggering in a circle, his breathing short and raspy, he cursed, prayed but then stalled, tumbled, and fell flat on his face, a large gust of dirt bellowed out from under him.

I groaned and rolled up to my knees, crawling over to Chavo, I saw the plunger end sticking out of the mangled eye. The rest of the syringe had buried itself deep in his brain. The one good eye looked upwards like something was stuck on his forehead. I felt for a pulse and found none within the thick folds of fat.

I grunted then pushed against the flab until my hand found the 9mm Chavo had fallen on. With a quick check of the magazine, I stuffed it in my waistband. I frisked Chavo over. I took the few bills from his wallet, crammed them in my pocket before limping over to the ladder and clambered up the rickety ladder.

Everything was bad timing.

Off in the distance, the sound of the Buick could be heard.

The staccato sound popping from the exhaust drew closer. I winced, staggering through the wreckage of boards and old furniture.

Luis rolled up in the Buick, a toothpick quivering in his mouth. I stayed within the shadows of the doorway as he got out holding the tray of drinks and a small bag of burgers. The drink tray only held two cups of Coke.

I stepped out into the bright sun just as he started to close the door with a booted foot. He paused. A look of concern began stretching across his face. He saw the blood trail from the wound near my hairline. I stood covered in dirt and dust from head to toe. I seethed with rage. The toothpick in his lips pointed straight out, clenched between clamped teeth. I slowly reached over for the handle on the 9mm. We both knew what was coming.

I pointed to the drink tray. "*Te olvidaste uno…amigo*," I said, pointing out the fact he forgot my drink.

He suddenly dropped the drink tray and food. They tumbled and splattered on the ground as he dove inside the Buick and grabbed the Red hawk. He blasted off a couple of rounds to get things started, but he was going for something bigger gun-wise.

I pulled the 9mm and threw myself behind a pile of rusty barrels.

THIRTY-FOUR

The bad thing about the 9mm is that it doesn't have enough ass to punch through a car door and do any kind of terminal damage. Sure, it'll bust through the out skin with no issue. But beyond that, the bullet starts to break up, becoming less effective. There's the glass, the window framework or, if the bullet is fortunate enough to have survived, it'll hit the inner door panel and inner skin in fragments.

I blasted a couple off. The slugs pounded the wobbling driver's door that Luis was crouched behind. I cursed with wide eyes when the barrel of an M4 came up over the door. A long burst thundered across the gap between us.

The copper-coated lead bounced off the barrels or punched through the wooden walls, throwing chunks of wood splinters and dust in all directions. He had no idea where I was. If he had half a brain and aimed a few inches lower, he would've nailed my ass. As it was, I was crab-crawling away along a long small indention that ran along the edge of the house. He was picking anything that might look like a threat and blasting away.

Cursing, I wiggled away from the dust storm of flying splinters and exploding earth. A barrage of .556 whined and flew in all directions. Then, as quickly as it had started, the sound of the M4 clicked. Luis cursed. He'd blown off an entire magazine. But in another few seconds, he'd be back in action after he reloaded.

I reared up just as Luis knelt to stuff in a fresh magazine. His curses were loud under the brim of his straw hat. I held aim with trembling hands and focused on his straw hat. He rose. The muzzle of my 9mm followed. The M4 swung up. I blasted off a half dozen rounds in rapid succession.

Luis' hat tumbled off his head, his arm flailed. The rifle still clutched in his right hand, went slack, the barrel end fell, and a long burst tore up the ground around him. He crumpled back into the dust cloud before settling against the rear wheel of the Buick.

I stood there for several minutes, realizing what I'd done. I wasn't taking any chances. I crouched, holding the 9mm up, finger ready on the trigger, and moved forward. The only sound was my breathing. I kept the sights on Luis' body, unsure if he was dead. If he popped up, he was going to get a face full of 9mm.

I cringed. There were several red welts on the cheek and nose. The welts leaked rich, red blood in thin rivulets down his face, across his neck, and dripped to the dry earth.

I cringed. *God damn*, I thought.

I blew Luis away in self-defense, but would the courts of the land see it that way? I had seen war at its worst, the ultimate failure of the human endeavor. Life and death struggle at the amusement of the rich and powerful. The difference here was I stood in the civilian world. I risked losing everything…literally. Killing someone bothered me now as it did then. Anyone who said killing never bothered them would be lying. I knew better. Pulling the trigger on someone is the absolute hardest thing anyone can do.

I stood shaking and looked around for God only knew what. Redemption? Maybe God was out there in the cold desert waiting for me to repent, something, but I saw nothing and received neither condemnation nor confirmation if I was right or wrong.

I shook it off. Get a grip, breathe in slow, I told myself.

I reached down, grabbed the M4, and slung it up over my shoulder. The keys dangled from the ignition. I leaned over Luis' corpse, grabbed them, and walked around to the trunk, and popped it open. Within the trunk were several bags. Grabbing one, the metallic ringing of tools rang out. Unzipping it, I saw multiple saws, cleavers, and a couple of axes. I looked over to Luis.

"You mother fuckers," I smiled. At least I felt a small wave of redemption in my killing the two of them. It was clear Luis had plans to carve up my carcass.

Within the other bag, I found several loaded magazines for the M4 and a box of 9mm. There were also multiple bundles. I saw what they were easy enough. I picked up one of the cellophane-wrapped bricks.

Cocaine.

I scooped out the ammo, took the bag, and shook the bundles out onto the ground. A few kicks and the bundles tumbled away. A single bundle burst open, the powder floating in the breeze. If anything, once the cops discovered the scene, it would be ruled a drug deal gone bad at first glance.

I took hold of Luis' booted feet and dragged him into the weeds, ignoring the trail of blood that followed him. I'd almost forgotten a critical item he had stuffed in his shirt pocket. I dug into it and took his cell phone. I grabbed up the ammo from the trunk, slammed it shut, tossing everything on the passenger seat. The Red hawk was the last gun to grab off the dusty floorboard.

I had no intentions of getting caught this time. With Luis and Chavo out of the picture, I could move freely, but I had to be quick in figuring out where the hell Enrique's compound was. I had an idea, but I had to move fast.

The minute I showed up, all hell would crack loose. I glanced over the guns and the small amount of ammo. It was pitiful, but it would be enough to achieve the goal. I didn't owe shit to Erika, but I needed to know what she knew and the critical key of where Jake and Erin were hiding. I just couldn't let that go.

I slid in behind the small chain steering wheel, fumbled with the ignition key for a moment before firing off the Buick. The rapid staccato from the exhaust rumbled to life. It picked up in tempo when I threw it in gear and ripped ass out of there in a cloud of dust.

THIRTY-FIVE

I counted four men on perimeter duty. They were moving in a set pattern. Every few minutes one or another would make a circuit around the area they were watching, pause, look around and shuffle back to their starting point. Scanning the buildings, I found another up in the barn loft opening and another man hid in the shadows of an open-faced metal shack some hundred yards from each other.

Six.

And they were armed with AK or AR variants.

I was sure there was more hidden out of sight.

Getting in there was going to be problematic. Lowering the binoculars, I looked overhead. The sun was an easy few hours away from settling on the horizon. I peered through the binoculars and studied the opposition.

Besides the large barn and the metal shack, there were several other buildings including a two-story adobe structure. I counted half-dozen trucks, including Enrique's Dodge, the two Chevys, and a Ford. There were several sedans scattered around the twenty-acre ranchette. All it meant was there were plenty of men and firepower. The two-story adobe house was the only logical choice for where they were keeping Erika. I doubted Enrique would be that cruel in keeping her anywhere else unless she was proving to be some kind of problem.

The main road leading up to the entrance also had its problems. Several hundred yards down the washboard dirt road was a beat-to-shit Ford Ranger pickup with two men in the back talking. The truck was positioned down a low dip in the ground, well out of sight from any incoming traffic. Each one had a pistol strapped to his waist. They also probably had radio contact with the main house. That would be an easy assumption. A guard at the entrance, the compound was well guarded and I was betting there were cameras, motion sensors, alarms at the weak points. I was betting Enrique was involved in plenty of other things, which was why he needed so many men and guns.

It'd taken me several hours to pinpoint this location. It was situated a good five miles off the main highway, nestled at the foot of the south end of the Manzano Mountains that spilled out onto the vast open barren plains. Belen could be seen as a spec in the distance by a good ten miles.

It was the only option out there. There were no other houses, cabins, or anything. A few dark spots of cattle dotted the vast rangelands were the only other inhabitants out here. I'd taken Highway 60 out of Mountainair up to Highway 47 and headed north toward Belen. I passed the compound, saw the dusty road leading up to it. A large double gate blocked anyone from going up the road. Signs hung off the fence declaring it was private property. The dead give-away was the arched wrought-iron sign over the double green gates. The fancy script declared itself to be '*El Armadillio*'. The same name Chavo had mentioned earlier at the diner.

Finding a back way in was a pain in the ass. Most of the ranchers had gates that were padlocked. I found a lone turnoff that was another five miles past the ranch. I assumed it was land belonging to BLM or the State of New Mexico. The road led within a few miles of the compound and dead-ended at the edge of a deep arroyo.

I gathered up the gear I needed. The M4 was the only gun I was taking in. I stuffed a mag of .556 in each back pocket but left the other guns in the trunk. I figured that would be enough. I took the binoculars and a couple of bottles of water from the trunk. Off in the distance, the compound shimmered within the heat waves like a deadly mirage.

Nestled within were men of violence willing to do bad things. I just hoped they hadn't done anything to Erika.

THIRTY-SIX

I hid down near the base of a lone cholla cactus tree nestled against the wall of the arroyo. I paused a few minutes, resting while taking a few swigs from the water bottle. I figured I had maybe an hour left before the darkness finished pushing the sun under the western horizon.

It took me awhile crawling up the arroyo. I rose and took a quick scope of the area. I was within fifty yards of the main two-story house. A balcony on the second story hung just over the arroyo. I figured Erika was in there...somewhere. Given Enrique might have some sense of aristocratic duty, he was keeping her comfortable. The first floor had a concrete pad and walkway that led up to a set of double doors.

My main avenue of entry.

I moved the binoculars around the compound. The men appeared much closer. The strains of boredom were scrawled on their faces. Sheer boredom. I caught one guard dozing in the metal shack. This should be a simple exercise. I enter through the patio doors maybe find a guard or two, possibly three moving around the interior. Enrique would be inside perhaps. His Dodge 4x4 was parked out front. So, five in total. A good number to start with.

I needed a diversion though. That would be ideal. I wasn't seeing the angle on how to go about it. The only option I had was to get inside the main house and use brute force. I had to move quickly and eliminate anyone in my way. If I managed to nail Enrique in the process it would be for the better.

I swept the compound again. I had the M4. Not much but it would have to do. All I had to do was wait for full dark before setting off the fireworks. Looking up to the blue and orange skies, I cursed mentally. I would have to wait for full dark. Eyeing the gate guards positioned near the entranceway, I saw a sudden flurry of activity. There were shouts of rage and surprise. Something was happening and in a bad way. The rest of the guards in the compound shifted into action.

An explosion rocked the compound. The men by the gate vaporized in a bloom of orange flame. The Ford truck lifted and spilled over on its side. The ground rippled, dust rose in waves, spreading. Men flew into action, while others staggered to their feet having been blown over like leaves in the wind. I crawled back up the embankment, holding the binoculars up. The dust cloud had thinned but from within, several shadows moved forward. At first, I thought there was an accident. Maybe one of the gate guards was playing with a grenade or something. But these men...there was something different about them. I had no idea who they were. Maybe they were a group of pissed-off ranchers, maybe they were the Law, or maybe local drug competitors.

I spat a chunk of dust.

If ever I was asking for a diversion, this was it.

Whoever they were, they weren't here for tamales, tequila, and good times. The middle man was tall, bulky-looking. He wore a long slicker jacket and an old-style western hat. He blasted a pair of old-time western era pistols clutched in each hand. The compound exploded in a flurry of gunfire and well-timed explosions. One of the invaders was blasting off with an old M79 grenade rifle, blasting shells into the nearby buildings and anywhere else the compound guards were hiding. The third man was blasting away with, of all things, a World War Two era Browning automatic rifle.

The trio fanned out, picking out any targets of opportunity. Men spun, died, yelled in agony or frustration, others in fear. Erika and I were in the middle of it. If I didn't get a move on, we would both end up dead.

I pushed myself up with a heavy grunt, M4 at the ready, and dashed for the back patio entrance.

THIRTY-SEVEN

I busted through the patio doors, sweeping the M4 side to side. A much older woman, fat, bulging in her white dress, cowered in the corner. She was just the maid or possibly the cook. I didn't give two shits who she was as long as she told me where Erika was. She made the sign of the cross. I knelt beside her, watching the entrance that opened into the main foray.

"Erika?" I whispered.

The woman blinked. The name registered in her eyes. She raised a trembling finger, pointing up the stairs at the end of the foray. I waved the M4 barrel. "*Vamanos.*"

She rose, took a long look in terror, and waddled off as quickly as she could for the side door.

I entered the main hall, following the M4's muzzle. I pointed the barrel to the top of the stairs. A guard was at the top. His eyes went wide, the AK 47 muzzle swung up. I took the shot. The burst ripped across his chest. The AK fell from his fingers. I kept the M4 pointing up at the top, moving quickly to the top landing, and stepped over the corpse. I ignored my feelings of regret.

I moved to the first door, the door was unlocked, I pushed it open. I poked the M4 in and followed, slicing the angles with the barrel. I heard a whimper from the closet, popped the door open. Erika was cowered in the corner. She stopped whimpering, opened her eyes and her jaw dropped.

I held out a hand. "C'mon! Let's go!" I shouted.

She took it, gathered her feet. "I thought..."

"No, I didn't forget about you."

"What took you so long?"

I pointed the M4 toward the door. "I had a couple of obstacles in the way."

I stepped out into the hall when a barrage of lead flashed and whipped past. Jumping back, I shoved the M4 out and let off a burst. I heard a scream, poked my head out in time to see a man crawling for the corner. A trail of blood leaked from his legs. Another man reached down to grab him. I instantly recognized the tattoos scrawled on the arm. I blasted off a barrage. Rico reared back, cursed a long string of obscenities in rapid Spanish. The bullets gouged the adobe walls, showering the crawling man in alabaster dust and plaster.

Rico snarled. Taking a chance, he extended his arm around the corner. The 9mm in his hand barked, popped, the rounds chewing chunks of adobe from the walls.

The front door below exploded open. A man cloaked in a trench coat and cowboy hat lumbered in. His features were dark against the backdrop of the setting sun. All I saw was the outline of a Browning automatic rifle. That alone put the fear of God into my soul.

Rico's eyes went wide and he shifted targets. I chose the better part of valor. I dove back in the room just as the explosive pops from Rico's pistol went to work. Erika was huddled down in the corner, hands over her ears.

The rolling rumble of automatic gunfire ripped through the air. The heavy slugs blasted holes in the walls. The light fixture overhead jangled, swinging from the barrage. I heard Rico screaming, shooting off a continuous burst from his 9mm quickly followed by the thunderclap from the BAR. Rico was dead. He just hadn't realized it. He screamed in agony, followed by gurgling sounds that were coming from the hallway. Heavy footfalls were moving up the stairs, then more explosive gunfire.

I grabbed Erika, shook her. "We got to go!"

She realized the situation. She nodded in understanding. I ran over to the balcony door and threw it open. The cool breeze of the oncoming night washed over my face. Down below was the edge of the arroyo. The dirt should be soft enough. A good fifty-yard run to the bend. Estimated time before the cowboy with the BAR started blasting us from the balcony? Maybe twenty, twenty-five tops. I slung the M4 across my back. Any effort was better than none.

"I can't do this," Erika looked over the edge of the balcony.

I clamored over the railing. "No time to debate," I said.

"Isn't there another way?" She looked at my shoulder, reached up to touch the wound. "You're hurt."

I looked over my shoulder. I hadn't noticed I had been grazed by a bullet or a chunk of debris. The angry furrow bled profusely, trailing down my arm. A shadow loomed outside the room.

"You first," I grabbed her arm, leaned over and grabbed her waist, and lifted her over the railing. She felt good at that moment. She grabbed my neck like a wet cat. "No, no, no, George, please don't let me go!"

I did my best to lower her down, but I lost my grip and she tumbled into a free fall. She let off a small shriek and hit the ground. An explosion of dust, a muffled curse, and Erika rolled to the bottom of the ditch. I dropped off the edge, hit the ground, and tumbled after her.

She rose, started to yell a long line of Spanish curse words. I lunged forward, grabbed her, and pressed both of us against the base of the wall of the arroyo. She struggled, clawing at my hand wrapped around her mouth. I wasn't taking any chances. Above, the muzzle of the BAR poked out over the railing. A rapid blast exploded overhead. Erika froze her eyes wide in sudden fear. I heard a distant scream from behind me.

One of Enrique's men must've had a change of heart. He tried running off toward the foothills. But it was a long run to attempt. I saw the guard tumble from the hill. If he had made the peak, he might've had a chance. As it was, his limp corpse rolled into a cluster of rocks near the arroyo's edge. The brown eyes drained of life fell upon us. His hand flopped over the edge. Another burst. The rounds splashed across the chest. There was more cackling laughter, and then the muzzle of the BAR disappeared.

We stayed silent. Erika looked at me, eyes wide. She shivered under the weight of my body on top of her. I rose, looking up to the balcony. The cowboy wasn't there. Erika crept up beside me, gripping my arm. "Are they gone?" She whispered.

"Hardly," I mumbled.

A sudden echoing burst rang out from deep inside the house. Enrique's men must've found enough courage to come out of hiding. A massive exchange of thundering pops and flashes bellowed from inside. Flinching, I grabbed Erika's hand. We ran along the ditch running for our lives.

THIRTY-EIGHT

Enrique's army came out on the short end of the stick. The gunfire had tapered off to a few sporadic pops before silence settled in. Looking carefully around the corner of the arroyo, were two corpses. I stopped, knelt over the corpses, patting them down for anything to help increase our odds of surviving. Neither one had anything of value. Somewhere a fire was raging. Thick plumes of smoke drifted across the ditch. I took the M4 off my shoulder, ejected the magazine, and dug the spare out of my back pocket. I blew off most of the dust and stuffed it in.

I still didn't know who the hell was hitting the compound. It sure wasn't the cops or the Feds. If it had been, we'd all been wearing those nice fancy stainless wrist bracelets by now. I moved the brush aside. The darkness had fallen but there was still enough light to make out the new players.

The cowboy strolled up to Enrique, the pistol held out ever so casually. Enrique was kneeling, clutching a damaged arm. He was cursing in Spanish, spitting chunks of phlegm. I hadn't the foggiest notion where Enrique was from the onset of this maelstrom. But it was obvious now that he had been caught. The cowboy cocked the hammer back on the pistol. Some words were exchanged. A second later a thunderclap rippled the air. I ducked down the ditch instinctively then slowly inched my way back up to the edge.

"Olsen!" The voice was deep, demanding. "George Olsen! You hear me, boy?"

I licked my lips. I didn't dare move. Just the sound of my breathing felt like I was being betrayed.

"Erika Fernandez!"

Erika froze, eyes clenched shut. The look of disappointment clouded her face.

"Fernandez?" I hissed. I had to know.

"What?"

"Arturo Fernandez, ring a bell?"

"My uncle," she whispered. "Why?"

I ignored the question and pressed in with my own. "Then you are Rubin Castillo's cousin?"

She nodded slowly. "He is. How did you know? Do you know him?"

"I know him," I grunted.

She started to say something else. I held a hand up cutting her off. "We'll talk in a bit." I inched my head up over the lip of the arroyo, peering through the dried clumps of prairie grass and yucca plants. The men stood surrounded by the light of the flames. The one with the BAR inserted another magazine, checked the chamber, and lifted it to his shoulder. The larger man in the middle held his pistol up. Man number three held an M79 grenade rifle. *Jesus...*

"You hear me?" The middle man shouted. "We know you're out there." He continued holding his pistol. "It's all good. The bad guys are dead."

Southern. The tones and accents were Southern, deep wholesome Southern. They weren't cops. They sure as hell weren't Cartel. The final options? Dixie Mafia.

Shiiiit!

"Who are they?" Erika whispered. The question was etched in fear.

"Bad people who want to do bad things," I wiped the grit and sweat from my forehead with the back of a hand. "Dixie Mafia, shit." The M4 shook in my hands. I could take a chance and maybe take the lot of them out, but that was far-fetched. These men were professional killers. Hell, they had just wiped out an army like they were *hors d'oeuvres.*

"Dixie Mafia?" Erika furrowed her eyebrows.

"It's a long story," I answered.

"What do we do then?"

The still of the night was rolling in. It was light enough to see the arroyo but dark enough in that it snaked its way through the barren landscape. The further away we got the better.

I pushed off the ditch bank wall. The man was yelling into the flames for Erika and me to give ourselves up. I wasn't kosher on that idea. "We run like hell. Let's go!"

She nodded and we moved at a run in a half-crouch position, making sure we stayed well below the arroyo's edge. We kept moving, the sound of violence and flames soon faded to the normal sounds of the desert plains. Behind us, the lights from the flames had engulfed the main house. We stopped once to catch our breath and to ease the burning muscles in our legs. After a few minutes of rest, we moved on. The Buick headlights reflected the lights from the far distant flames.

I popped the trunk open, grabbed a couple of water bottles, handing one to Erika. I drank every drop and tossed the bottle before grabbing another. Erika did the same.

"You drive," I said, popping the passenger door open.

She didn't argue and slid in behind the wheel.

She fumbled with the keys before the Buick rumbled to life. I saw a series of rapid flashes, followed by the echoing clap from somewhere behind us. The back window exploded. Erika screamed and floored the gas pedal in a violent reaction. I grabbed the M4, stabbed it out the passenger window, and let cut loose with a long burst. The sounds of bullets impacted the car panels, but Erika gassed the Buick down the dirt road away from the thundering death that followed.

THIRTY-NINE

We took the road to Belen. It must've been low rider night. We merged onto the main drag and the road was flooded with meticulously clean machines with glaring, bright paint jobs and hydraulic systems. We stopped at the red light. An old Monte Carlo was perched on three wheels beside us. I was always amazed by what those works of art could do. It took my mind off of our current problems. Any other time, I might've stopped and watched.

The passenger took a long look over the Buick. By this point, the Buick had a good number of bullet holes in it. The rear window was shot out and it was covered in a heavy coat of dust and mud. Erika and I were tired. I know all I wanted was a hot shower, a cold beer, and about two days of sleep. The M4 was out of sight.

"What the fuck happened?" The passenger laughed. "What a

shitty ride, *ese*."

I looked over.

The pudgy passenger suddenly frowned. He must've seen my expression, maybe the blood and dirt caked on my face. Or maybe I was not in the mood for bullshit. "She's a wild ride, what can I say?" I yelled with a smile.

He smiled, looking Erika over, nodding his approval.

The light turned green and Erika blushed. "I'm a wild ride? Wouldn't you like to know?"

I looked forward. "The car, Erika, I was referring to the car."

She looked over with a frown. Our eyes met and suddenly we burst into giggles and laughter. It was a good release. We needed it considering the hell we'd come from.

I reached in the back, fumbling around the back seat. I found my medic kit, plopped it on my lap, unrolling it. The shoulder injury had settled into a dull pulsating throb. I took my water bottle and doused it clean.

Erika glanced over, curiously studying the way I was operating on the injured limb. I numbed up the area with a few pokes with a syringe filled with Lidocaine. I then flushed the area out with sterilized water. Once the flesh had settled into a dull throb, I began sewing it with the stitching kit.

"Where'd you learn how to do that?" Erika asked.

"Military," I mumbled.

"I had a feeling."

"I was a medic," I finished the stitch job, cut the thread, and repacked the kit bag. I lit up a cigarette, rolled down the window wishing to change the subject. I had broken enough Marshals rules today that it wouldn't matter if I broke one more.

"Looks like you would've made a good doctor."

"I thought about that at one time."

"But you became a diesel mechanic instead?"

I smiled. "Trucks don't scream in pain when you're trying to fix 'em."

I looked away, staring at the dark shadowy blurs of pinion trees and shrubbery.

"Can I ask you something, George?"

I chuffed out a cloud of smoke. "Must be pretty important."

She looked over, wearing a serious expression. "What's your real name?"

I looked at her for a minute and then back out the dusty windshield. "Why ask that?"

Enrique said that wasn't your real name."

"George is my real name, Erika."

She knew I was lying. "You'll never tell me, will you?"

"I can't."

"Will you tell me when this blows over?"

"Maybe."

She looked away, watching the road. I could tell she wasn't happy with the answer. I didn't trust her even though she had held up through everything at this point. Maybe I was confused between her and Jill. Maybe God was telling me to move off from the old life, take up a new road.

But I knew God had a weird, twisted sense of humor.

We rode in silence, passing through Los Lunas before merging onto I-25 through Albuquerque. We were taking the long route around back to Moriarty. There was no way the Dixie Mafia boys would start shit anywhere near the population. If we had gone the other way through Mountainair, they could have ambushed us easily. There was plenty of open space and very little traffic. We merged onto I-40, headed back toward Moriarty. The only thing I had to worry about was getting pulled over by some unassuming cop. We stopped once. I checked the lights and everything. Miraculously, they all worked. We shoved off again, gliding down I-40 in silence.

So, I'm in deep shit, I'm thinking. The chill of night edged away the warm air blowing into the windows. My thoughts were calculating what to do next besides go talk with Jake. One: the Feds...they were coming, eventually, and once they found out I was in the mix, it was a sure bet there would be plenty of prison time involved. Two: the Dixie Mafia was now in the picture and in a big way. It was evident that a war was in motion with the Mexican Cartel boys. They had thoroughly wiped out the Mexicans with hardly any effort. The Cartel wasn't going to let that slide. In a matter of days, there would be an army flooding into the Estancia Valley.

Erika was problem number three. Just a small town broad looking for a way out and not finding it. Or maybe she was just oblivious to everything swirling around us. Her name alone had condemned her to this chapter in her life. Sure she probably could've made better choices in life but who hadn't? Everybody in life makes the wrong moves. But, she did know something.

"I gotta ask," I said.

She looked over, eyes full of question marks. "Ask what?"

"Did you tell Enrique anything?"

She looked out the windshield, gripping the wheel harder. The muscle in her jaw flexed. "Nothing."

"So you talked about something?"

"No," she focused on the road. "We did, actually, but about my uncle."

"Your uncle?"

"Arturo Fernandez."

We didn't say anything more as we glided through Moriarty and down Highway 41.

Solution? None to be found.

"You're quiet?" Erika asked, stealing the occasional glance from the dark road rolling under us.

"I was thinking," I said. "That I used to live around here."

She looked back to the road. "Here?"

Studying the road and landmarks I saw it. The old Conoco sign had faded to a ripe yellow stain on the side of the road. It was faded even more so from the last time I had seen it. The headlights of the Buick bought out the last vestiges of color under the dim lights. "Make a turn here," I said.

She made the turn. A cluster of run-down mobile homes lined both sides of the battered road. After a few miles, the homes gave way to open rangeland. The darkness of night flooded the interior. Erika turned the wheel, avoiding the numerous potholes and or slowed down going over washboard ripples.

"Why are we going down this road again?" Erika looked over. The concern on her face was illuminated by the dash lights.

"Got to see if my pack is still there," I said.

"Pack?"

Looking at her, I wondered if she should be involved any further. "My money."

FORTY

It only took a few minutes to figure out where I used to live. I braced myself for the fact that the money might not even be there. The Buick rolled up on the prairie land. The headlights searching for anything I might recognize, but nothing struck a chord of recognition. I was half-expecting to see my old camper and Chevy truck still sitting there, waiting for me to return, but they were long gone.

The Buick stopped. I got out slowly, looking around, feeling the strange vibe of being a trespasser. I shut the door and limped away into the desert land. Erika killed the ignition and the lights on the Buick. The only sounds were the breeze rustling through the dead weeds and nearby power lines. Erika moved through the weeds, holding one of those cheap key-chain flashlights that can be found in any auto parts store. She stood beside me looking around like I was.

"Arturo Fernandez is your uncle," I said.

She shivered. "I said that already."

"Doesn't mean it doesn't mean something."

She looked puzzled. "If you mean he was part of that gang of bad cops, I don't believe it."

"You think he was falsely accused?"

She went silent, looking at the ground. "I don't know."

"I had a buddy who'd tell you differently."

"My uncle was *not* a bad man."

"What'd you tell Enrique?"

"Why?"

"He was after you, not me...not at the beginning anyway." I walked over to the spot where the camper once sat. Nature had reclaimed what was once mine and not much was left. A crumpled, faded beer can lay nestled in the silt sand, a broken fragment from a whiskey bottle, and a few other minor things were all that remained of a life long ago.

"Why me?" She moved up to me.

"You know something, Erika. Don't bullshit me. Your uncle told you something didn't he?"

"No...well," she hesitated. "He told me about some old family land."

"Family land?"

"He signed over some land to me just before he went to prison. He told me to never tell anyone and to make sure I kept up on the taxes."

"Where?"

"Someplace called Pines...Pinos...or something like that."

"Pinos Wells?"

She nodded. A breeze caught a tussle of her hair. She raked it back, holding it in place while she watched me. "Does it mean something?"

I looked over where my old shed had been. There was nothing left but a pile of bleached gray rotten boards. "Pinos Wells," I whispered. "Did you tell Enrique this?"

She shook her head. "I've never been out there. I don't even know where it's at."

"But, did you tell Enrique?"

"No, I swear. I knew it might mean something, but I didn't want anyone to know."

The dots were connecting. All along, everyone assumed Richardson was the only man who knew where the money was stashed. Everyone knew he took his secret of the location of the money to the grave. But, there was Arturo Fernandez, disgraced State of New Mexico cop who knew where Richardson had stashed the money. He might even have helped Richardson hide the stash.

I tried recalling all the information from Richardson's family tree that dated back to Pinos Wells. Information was foggy at best, but it left me wondering if Arturo's family was around at the same time frame. Now, if that angle was true? Then I had something to go on. But, there was no way I could go poke around Pinos Wells, not right now. Not only was the Cartel looking but the Dixie Mafia was around. Add in the extra spice of the FBI and potentially the US Marshals? It was a perfect recipe for disaster.

"How much land?" I asked.

"I don't know how much but it's a lot," she said.

Then there was Erin and his boyfriend club of idiots. I expressed my concerns to Erika. "You realize Erin, Bob, and Jake are tied up with this? They kidnapped you back to hand both me and you over to the Dixie Mafia in a package deal."

She frowned. "I'm afraid of that. I think they weren't my friends after all. Not after they shot that man Diego on Highway 41."

I flashed the light on her. "So let get this story right. First, you're kidnapped by the Cartel, then Erin and his crew managed to pull over Diego in his lowrider."

"Diego was moving me to another safe house for the Cartel. I was blindfolded and tied up in the back seat. I'm not sure what happened next, but Diego pulled over the side of the road, told me to stay quiet. He stepped out and all I heard was a few gunshots. It scared the hell out of me."

"Erin and his crew see you're in the back seat and take you away, right?"

"Exactly. I should've known something was wrong when they wouldn't let me call my family to let them know I was okay."

"They were waiting for me to show up. I'm not sure how they knew I was coming but I suspect," I held up a finger. "I suspect one of them was ratting out to the Cartel. The question is was it Erin or Jake."

Erika shivered. "You think so?"

"You all worked together, right?"

"We did, we all met a few months ago, and they seemed like cool guys to hang out with, well, except Erin. He was always trying to get more out of me other than work things."

I gave a small grin. "Always?"

"Every time. He was always hitting on me."

"They knew who you were, and they were keeping you close for the right moment, but instead, you got kidnapped by the Cartel before they could act."

"What moment was that?"

"The moment I would come back like an idiot. We will be talking to Jake."

"Jake?"

"He and Erin are the only survivors. When we got ambushed

out in the cornfields, Erin was just too damned scared. I don't believe he was the Cartel snitch. Jake though?" I looked up to the night skies. "He knows something more to this, which is why, when we're done here, we're going to pay him a visit." I moved the light around.

"Is that necessary?"

"I believe it is."

"What about this money then?" Erika said.

Looking back, I held the beam on her. She looked cold, standing there with her arms folded across her midsection. The light breeze played with the ends of her long black hair. "Right when this shit first kicked up, I had a backup plan, but I never got to push it into motion."

The beam bounced around across the field. The old busted-up shed was no longer standing but the concrete foundation could be seen. Walking over to the broken woodpile, I poked the light out to my left and down. Hidden in the weeds was a large circular cover.

"Who are you?" Erika asked.

I walked over to the pump house cover, knelt, and slid it back. Poking the light down through the maze of thick cobwebs and spider nests, the dirt floor looked undisturbed.

"I told you. George, George Olsen," I answered.

"I have my doubts about that. Enrique mentioned a Logan Pierce. Are you him?"

I snorted, choking off a laugh. "Not even close."

"This isn't funny at all. You're making fun of me."

I shrugged, swung a booted foot down the edge, feeling my toe catch the first ladder rung. "Believe what you want."

I moved down the ladder until, twelve-foot down, my feet rested on the floor. I swept away the cobwebs. Spiders scurried away from the light. I knelt beside the ladder footing and began digging away at the soft soil. After several minutes, my fingers raked across something solid. I cleared away the dirt, exposing something that was dull black. I smiled. It was that familiar feeling I had years ago when Logan and I had found the original cache of money out on Musgrave's ranch.

I pulled the bag free from the dirt, beat the dust from it. Age and the dry soil had sucked the life out of the canvas material. Carefully tucking the rotten canvas sack under my arm, I clambered back up the ladder. I slammed the rotten bag down on the lid and began dusting myself off.

There was no point attempting in playing with the zipper. I ripped the fabric apart. The bundles of dried plastic still held their shape. I took a knife and split the plastic and Benjamin Franklin's face appeared.

Erika gasped. "This can't be the money everyone is looking for? What a pitiful amount."

I smiled, looking up at her. "No, just a very small piece of it, and we're going to need it." I fumbled with the wrapping on the main package and felt the familiar shape. I ripped it open revealing a towel that still looked fresh. Unwrapping the bundle, my old Taurus .357 tumbled out. It gleamed as if I had just put it there yesterday. Checking the cylinder, the rounds were still present. Tucking it away in my waistband, I snatched up the bundle of musty cash.

"Let's bogey, young Lass," The night was still young, but a plan was formulating in my mind.

"What's the plan?" Erika muttered in concern.

I tossed the bundle up in the air, caught it in the other hand. "How should I know? I'm making all this up as we go, but I got a grain of an idea."

FORTY-ONE

We took a right turn off Highway 41 onto Marshals Road and headed west. After a half-hour of bouncing down the washboard and pothole-infested road, we came out on CR337 and turned south before turning on some goat trail marked CR 53. The trail opened up to a well-maintained gravel road. Erika pointed out that Jake's house was only a mile or so up the road. When we were within a few hundred yards, I told her to kill the lights and stop.

We hid behind a large knoll with a cluster of small pines sprouting from the top. I took up my binoculars, hopped out of the Buick, and jumped the fence. I pushed through the pine scrub, made my way to the peak of the low hill, raised my binoculars, and scanned the distant ranch house. Even under the moon of night, there was enough light to see the outbuildings, a barn, and a cluster of rotting trucks and farm equipment scattered across the property. The main house was lit up and told me that Jake or someone was home.

I dug the cell phone out of my pocket, flipped it open. It was time to push my plan into action. I punched in the number for Lane's phone. I grudgingly knew it by heart due to the number of times I had to call him.

The phone buzzed a few times before the line picked up. "Marshal Lane," the reply was blunt.

"Lane, this Olsen."

He was silent, then. "God damn it, Olsen, I warned you the last time!"

"I know, I know, look, I was forced up here, understand that first off."

"You should've called."

"You got rats in your house," I didn't wait for him to replay. "Where are you?"

"Albuquerque, weird coincidence in that we were looking for you anyway. We figured you came back here."

"I'm going to hand it all to you, lock stock and barrel, but I'm not dealing with anyone from your clown posse. You come here alone."

"Where?"

I dug the notes I scribbled on a piece of paper out of my pocket. "Out in the middle of nowhere. From Highway 41, take Marshals Road," I grunted. "Imagine the irony of that name, anyway, keep going for about twenty miles until you hit a fork and head left. You should see a Buick. We'll be there."

"Stay put, we're coming," Lane replied.

"Alone, Lane, don't fuck this up, I'm serious."

"What the hell are you doing?"

"Gathering up the proof. You come up here with anyone else and we're gone." I tossed the phone off in the weeds. Lane was protesting, but he had more than enough time to track the device. I didn't see a need for the drop phone any longer.

I scanned the compound again. The first part of the plan was in motion. Lane was probably already hauling ass code blue to Moriarty. Time was of the essence. If I played this right, I had a chance of coming out of this in one piece and with little if any prison time. Erika would be safe, Jake and Erin would end up getting married to the man with the most cigarettes at some shit-hole Federal prison. Jill would be scooped up, and even though she might not like it, would be forced into the WITSEC program. I pass off all the info to the Marshals. Everyone safe, bad guys put away, and life moves on. At least that was what I was hoping for. Beer, broads, and touchdowns.

I wondered if Erin was hiding here also. After he had split from the carnage of wreckage in the cornfield, no one had seen him anywhere. It was a slim chance, but he might've hidden here along with Jake. I moved away from the hilltop and went back to the Buick. Erika watched me with concern. I slid back into the passenger seat, instructing her to roll out but to keep the headlights off. When we were within fifty yards, I told her to pull off the road.

I took up the M4 from the back seat and popped the door open. Erika took hold of my arm.

"What are you planning to do?"

"A friendly discussion," I grabbed the medic bag.

She placed a hand on mine. "That gun is not friendly."

"I'm going to get answers so we can both get out of this alive. You understand, right?"

"Please don't hurt him," she pleaded. "It'll just make things worse."

I stepped out, flicked the cigarette butt end over end down the dirt trail. Pulling back the charging handle, the moonlight reflected off a brass cartridge nestled within the bore. "Considering the mess we came from this is a small matter." I slung up the medic bag.

Before she could protest, I moved off into the brush. The property was surrounded by thick clusters of pine and scrub oak and dead, waist-high weeds sprouted everywhere. I veered to the left and circled until a wire fence was seen. I squatted on my haunches, peering off toward the main house which was ablaze in light.

The sounds of chickens clucking came from the coop. I saw several cows meandering around the property, chewing at the dead weeds and grass. I hadn't seen or heard any dogs moving around or barking. That was a good thing. I didn't like the idea of killing a man's best friend. The chickens were still raising hell near a coop. A light flickered on. Jake stood out in the center of the chicken pen, clothed in nothing but a pair of underwear scattering chicken feed. I waited for him to move away, and once he did, I crawled under the wire.

At a half-crouch, I ran for the nearby barn, knelt by the corner. A horse moved away from the corral. A strong odor of decay reached my nostrils. I looked back to the corrals wondering where the dead animal was. Jake tossed out more chicken feed. He was humming a tune.

The stench only grew stronger when I moved into the barn. So much so, I had to pull the shirt neck over my nose to keep out the worst of it. I figured a dead horse or cow. The sound of flies buzzing intensified. I crouched low, making my way to the open barn doors on the far end. Jake waddled past the open barn doors, disappearing around the corner.

I stopped near a large pile of manure. I swatted away at the buzzing flies and gnats. Once the sound of Jake's footfalls faded, I rose and saw something sparkle in the pile of old manure. The familiar ring gleamed under the moon. The hand was stiff, rigid, and skin was drawn tight over the bones. There was no point in checking for vitals. Erin was under the pile of rotting hay and manure. He'd been lying there for the better part of two days. The flies buzzed incessantly over the exposed parts of his corpse, lapping up the remaining vestiges of moisture.

I shifted over beside the barn door, peering out. Jake moved around in the well-lit shed. I cinched up the M4, crouched low, and sprinted to Jake's house.

FORTY-TWO

Jake waddled through the door. I was seated in the dark corner of the living room. I held the M4 on him as he entered. He was humming a tune while he opened the fridge and bent over. He stood up, cracking open a can of Coors. Then he moved over to one of the overhead cabinets. A door swung open.

"You might want to grab one for me too, Jake."

He jumped, startled, looked around. He narrowed his eyes to slits looking into the dark living room. "Who's…?"

"Olsen," I stated flatly.

"Olsen..." his voice dropped to a whisper, eyes flickering in recognition.

I flicked on the light from the lampshade on the end table next to me. I made sure he saw the M4 was pointed at him. "I see you and

Erin had a bit of a falling out."

Jake slowly approached the living room, still clutching the can of Coors in one hand and a glass in the other.

"He's pretty ripe, you know?"

The Coors can trembled within his hand.

"You owe an explanation," I said.

"I owe you jack-shit."

"Turn around."

He stood there, silent.

I rose from the chair. "I said, turn around."

He turned ever so slowly like he was rotating with the speed of the earth.

I made it quick. I walked over, and with the butt of the rifle, I slammed him in the back of his melon head. He crumpled quick to his knees, the can of Coors splashed across the carpet. I grabbed his arms and zip-tied them together behind his back. With a hard shove, he fell face-first to the floor where I zip-tied his feet together. He was wheezing breathless gasps like he'd run a quarter-mile race. "What now? Kill me?"

"Answers, Jake, to life's great mysteries."

"I got money!" He started yelling between gasps.

"I bet you do, but first," I seated in the chair next to him. "Who you dealing with?"

He licked his lips. "I can't tell you that!"

I leaned over, jammed the barrel of the M4 between his legs. The fabric of the underwear clinched up. "I swear," I said. "I will blow your balls off."

"No, you won't."

I looked up. Erika stood there, arms folded. Her brown eyes looked at me with a firm tone. "There have been enough people killed over this."

"Erika, I said to wait..."

"In the car, yes, I know, but I'm making sure you don't."

I groaned and went back to Jake whose ass-cheeks were still clenched around the barrel of the rifle. "Who you working for?"

When I saw he wasn't going to answer, I punched him on the side of his mouth. Erika gasped. Jake began laughing in grunts.

I wasn't in the mood for it and punched him again.

"Percy Mills," he giggled. Bloody bubbles speckled his lips.

"Percy Mills?" I whispered. I pulled the M4 out of his ass, leaned back, lost in thought.

"You are so dead, Hendricks." He spat out a chunk of bloody phlegm. "It is best you let me loose. They're looking for you, you know?"

I ignored his threat. "Who's Percy Mills?"

He smiled. Blood-coated teeth flashed through broken lips. "The man who's going to kill you and your buddy Logan, and that bitch Amy…unless *you* tell me where that money is."

"I didn't come back here for the money. I was 'forced' back here." I wandered around the living room. A computer was on in the far corner. The desk was covered in papers. I casually glanced over the papers and saw several photographs. I reached over, picked one up. A familiar face starred back. It was several years old, maybe five tops but it was me. Stamped on the back was the official US Marshals logo. I shot a look back to Jake. His eyes rolled and he laid his head down on the carpet. The other photograph was of Jill and me. I picked up another of Logan and Amy.

"Where'd you get this?" I held up the photograph.

"Come look at this!"

Erika was in the kitchen. She stared at the cabinet. I walked into the kitchen. The cabinet was stacked with bundles of money, all neatly stacked on top of each other.

I took hold of a bundle.

"Is this the money?" She whispered.

I didn't believe it was. I opened another cabinet. There was another stack of money, not as much as the first cabinet, but enough to convince me Jake was getting paid to do something. "What's this?"

Jake didn't say anything, but the hate was welling up in his eyes.

"So…." I slowly paced back into the living room. "You were hoping to find the money, or at least get a cut, then turn yourself over to the Marshals. At least I'm thinking." I pointed a finger at him. "Who's your contact?"

"I ain't telling you shit!" Jake screamed.

"I don't think you understand my point," I paused, lit up the cigarette. I blew a cloud of smoke in his face. "Here it is, you, fat fucking Jake, with a brain the size of a fucking walnut. You think, or thought, that your buddies killed by the Cartel, then me, that all you had to do was go turn yourself in and escape with this money?"

He sat there like a kid, nostrils flaring, eyes began to tear up but he wasn't saying anything.

I tried another approach. I took several bundles from the kitchen cabinet, walked back into the living room. The fireplace dared me to start a fire. I tossed it in. On the mantel was a bottle of starting fluid. I popped the cap and gave the bundle a healthy dose. Looking over my shoulder, Jake lurched forward tight against the zip ties. "You wouldn't!"

I tossed in another bundle. "Tisk, tisk, Jake. It's dirty money. Blood money that the Cartel gave you, right?" I grabbed another bundle, shook it at him. "Or Dixie Mafia? Maybe both?" I tossed the second bundle in with the other.

"I figure, and this part is my fault, that you fed someone I knew down there in Monahans some bullshit info to get me to come back up here," I inhaled on my cigarette and blew a cloud. "Someone in the

Marshals told you where I was, right?" I took out my lighter and struck the flame.

He licked his lips. The desperation flickered in his eyes, sweaty forehead and all. I had him and I was guessing right. "You don't understand," he whispered. "Don't, please."

"A name?"

His eyes darted around like a pinball. "If I say anything, I'm a dead man."

"Last chance," I thumbed the lighter. A small flame flared to life.

"Some guy down in Monahans, some guy I was told worked with you," he croaked while hanging his head in resignation.

"No name?" I said with a puzzled expression.

Jake shook his head. "We just called him The Mexican."

"Do you know him?" Erika looked equally puzzled.

I didn't bother answering her question and focused on Jake who sat there like a scalded kid. "Did you meet him?"

He raised his head, shaking his head, eyes tear-stained. "He made me an offer to help him. The other guy was US Marshals, I never saw him directly but he always paid cash!"

I looked at the money pile. "So, where did all this come from?"

"From Percy and the Cartel," he groaned.

"You were playing both sides of this," I stood up and went over and grabbed a handful of hair.

"Do you realize what you've done?" I wanted to blast him, right in the forehead, but I knew it would only make my situation more unstable. Jake needed to be alive. That was the regrettable part. If he died, no one would believe anything.

"Stop..." she whispered.

I let go of his hair, staggered back, muttering. "Mills, Mills,

Percy Mills." I tried remembering all the Dixie Mafia material I could remember but was drawing a blank until I remembered a name. I turned back to Jake, he had pulled his knees up to his chest, bracing for another onslaught. "Did he have a relative named Hobart?"

He shook his head, his chest heaved. "I don't know, I was told to bring you in so they could squeeze you for the location of the money. Something about the money and resolving family squabbles."

"The Cartel?" I asked.

He shook his head. "I knew Diego from working the County Line. He was a mechanic, claiming he was Cartel," he hung his head again. "He offered a big chunk of money too."

"Jesus, Jake," Erika whispered. "You got me kidnapped! By the Cartel!"

There's an old German proverb. Too many cooks spoil the stew. The old saying held truth. In the beginning, it was just Logan and me. I didn't want any more guys involved because no one could truly hold a secret under wraps. In this case, Erin's merry band of wanna-be badasses were pawns for the Dixie Mafia. Diego was a part of Erin's group, even worked together, but he had his agenda going with the Cartel.

Diego was making deals with the Cartel, hell, he worked for them. It was all fine and dandy until Diego got waxed outside Estancia. The Dixie Mafia was playing Erin and his crew. They had probably offered big money and maybe some notoriety within the Mafia.

Instead of killing Jake in retaliation, the Cartel paid him a chunk of dough. They realized Erika was a key in helping them find the money. I come wandering into the picture and everyone lost their shit. Jake played both sides, hoping to walk away with a nice fat stack of dough. But there was a third group within the shadows. I was sure I knew who.

I grabbed the photographs off the desk. "Who's the other man?"

He looked confused. "What?"

"He's told us everything," Erika said.

I shook my head. "No, no, no. He hasn't."

Jake winced. "Okay, there's a guy, he said he was from the Feds."

"Does he look like a reject cast member from the TV show Miami Vice? With graying blonde hair?"

Jake looked up at, frowned. His eyes were full of question marks. "No?"

"Who, then?"

"I don't know their names," he licked his lips. "They gave me a number, had badges, official-looking. The deal was I turn you over to the Cartel. They gave me a name, some money, and had me call that guy down in Monahans. Some guy we called The Mexican. He said he worked with you."

"Who is he talking about?" Erika asked.

I frowned, sat in the chair, the M4 hung limp in my hands. I didn't want to believe it. Everything I had figured on had turned out to be wrong. "Manny...and your cousin, Rubin," I whispered. I cursed. Someone within the Feds had passed info off to the Cartel. Jake was just a tool in the scheme of things. It was a sure bet, one side or the other was going to put him down for a dirt nap. It was he hadn't realized what he was doing.

I clutched the papers in one hand. My life was just torched before my very eyes all because of the money. The root cause of all of this mess. I lamented my old life. The worst part was now Logan and Amy were sucked into it and they didn't even realize it. They were in imminent danger. I stumbled out the door, Erika trailed behind, protesting. "What does it mean?

I looked at the fistful of papers. I could vomit a mile. I looked up to Erika. "Go away," I whispered.

She grabbed my arm. "What is wrong? What's he saying?"

"It's bad, Erika. It's bad and it's only going to get worse. It would be best if you ran away, please for the love of God and all that's Holy, just leave."

Erika froze but her eyes were on something else. I spun, the hairs rose on my neck.

Lane stepped out of the shadows, hand on his service pistol.

FORTY-THREE

Lane pulled his service pistol. He pointed at me. "Drop the rifle, Olsen."

"Well, look who decides to show his fucking face!" I yelled. "You fucking traitor!"

Lane looked confused. "What the hell are you talking about? Drop the rifle," he held up the Glock. "I'm only warning you once."

"You and the Marshals sold us out."

Lane looked confused. "Sold…out?"

I held up the fistful of papers and photographs. "This, you fucking idiot!"

His eyes narrowed, confusion clouding over, but the Glock was steady in his hand. "Put it down and back away."

"You!" I yelled. "Cheap, fucking dime-store bastard!" I threw the papers and photographs at him. The papers fluttered to the ground.

He held the Glock up. "I'm ordering you to back away and put it down!" He eyed the M4 over my shoulder. "Drop the rifle...slow!"

"IN HERE!" Jake screamed out.

Lane was more confused. "What the hell is going on? Kidnapping now?"

I wish I had shot Jake in his nuts. I moved my hand slowly to the sling over my shoulder.

Lane lunged forward, jamming the pistol in my face. "I mean it, Olsen. One wrong move and I'll drop you where stand."

I pinched the strap with two fingers, slid it over my arm. I held it out and then let it fall. The M4 clattered to the ground with a heavy thud.

"Back away! Both of you!"

I took two steps back. Erika did the same.

"THANK GOD! THE COPS!" Jake yelled.

Lane ignored Jake. He held his pistol and bent down. With a free hand, he reached for the papers and held one up. His jaw working and his face flushed.

I held my hands up. "Don't tell me you didn't know!"

"No…" he whispered. He dropped the papers, stood up. "Turn around and place your hands on top of your head!"

"Face it, Lane, you got dirty people working for you," I turned, still holding up my hands.

"Drop to your knees!"

I got down on my knees. There were sounds of other people moving out in the brush. The snapping of dead weeds and twigs reached my ears. "You didn't come alone."

He blinked.

"Let me guess, you bought the whole squad with you?"

He held the Glock with steady hands. His breathing rate increased. "I came alone."

"All these papers mean we...Logan, Amy, and I have been compromised."

The sound of handcuffs jingled.

"I've never lied to you, Lane."

A voice from far off bellowed. "He's right."

Lane spun, the Glock stabbing the dark. I whirled and stood up. Brock stepped out into the light. He pointed a finger at me. "You stay there, dumb shit."

The sound of feet hammered the earth around the compound. I tried staring in the darkness. I saw a couple of shadows shift but knew there were more men out there. I looked down. The M4 lay on the ground. Its worn finish was dusty, old looking. I only had one thirty-round mag ready to go. Every bullet would have to count for something.

Lane's face was a mask of confusion. "Who are these guys?"

Brock smiled. "We have to talk, Lane."

I was ready to go out blazing in a hail of lead and take a few with me or kill whoever was out there. I gave Lane a quick nod and a half-smile. "They're your people."

FORTY-FOUR

Brock stepped in closer, his hands held up. Jake was screaming his head off. Erika took hold of my bicep. She wasn't sure what was going on but had a good idea that nothing was looking good. I kept my eyes focused in the dark. I counted three men at least. One shadow shifted behind the chicken coop. The chickens were raising hell. Another man was somewhere around the corrals by the barn. Number three was off ahead, behind Brock. I wasn't sure where but he was out there close to the fence line.

Lane stepped out, holding the Glock out in front of him.

"What the fuck you doing?" I yelled. "Get back here!"

Lane kept moving forward, ignoring my protests. "Brock!"

Brock continued holding his hands up. "Lane, lower your weapon and we'll talk."

"What the fuck is going on?" Lane pressed.

"Lane!" I yelled. "They ain't your buddies no more!"

"Shut up, Olsen!" Lane spat.

I could see a smile spread across Brock's face. "It's a complicated deal, Lane. Lower your pistol and we'll talk."

"Not until you explain what the hell's going on."

Jake continued screaming at the top of his lungs. Brock had enough. "Shut the hell up in there!"

Jake paused. "Brock? That you? Come get me out of these cuffs!"

"Now you be still in there, Jake. We're just having a discussion out here."

"No! Get me the fuck out of this!"

"Don't make me come in there, Jake," Brock started yelling. "If I do, I will beat your ass senseless! Now shut the hell up!"

Lane shook his head. "You know the guy inside?"

"I said it was complicated. What'd you expect? Do you think you can win this one? I got an army behind me, c'mon, man, lower the pistol."

"You…" Lane took a step forward, every muscle bunched up in rage. "You, sold out? Did you sell out information?"

"I'm just an errand boy, Lane. This thing... it's a lot bigger than both of us."

"Errand boy? I got a stack of papers compromising Federal witnesses!" He pointed at the papers on the ground.

Brock shuffled a foot in front of him like he was erasing something in the dirt. "It's for a lot of bigger people involved in a lot of things beyond both our understandings."

"Don't believe a word he says!" I yelled.

Lane snapped an angry look my way. "Olsen, I swear, if you open your mouth one more time, I'm going to shoot you in the face!"

He held the pistol steady on Brock.

"All we got to do is clean this mess up," Brock said while he nodded toward me. Then to Erika. "And her."

Lane looked back at me. Confusion, anger, and disbelief were etched across his face.

"Let's face facts," Brock continued. "This guy's been a pain in our ass from day one. The only saving grace is that we're on the trail where that money is located but we got orders to tie up loose ends."

"Loose ends…orders..." Lane's voice trailed off. I could tell he was in disbelief but the question was which way he was thinking. He rolled his head back and looked at me.

"Olsen is right about one thing though," he snapped his head back to Brock. "He hasn't lied about anything. Put your hands up!"

The shadows shifted, I settled on the closest target, sweat beaded on my forehead. I inched forward, readying myself to grab up the M4. Brock looked at me realizing I was a viable threat.

"I was hoping you'd understand," he looked at me. "But I guess that's no longer the case."

The seconds ticked by, silence fell in place, God was sweating, and the air was thick with the cloud of impending violence. It wasn't long and Brock made his move. He cleared leather in a blur. His own Glock barked, followed by the shadows behind him moving forward. Lane returned fire, forcing Brock to dive for cover behind an old derelict of a pickup. I grabbed Erika and shoved her down while scooping up the M4.

Shouts erupted across the compound and sparks of quick light and explosions erupted. A geyser of dirt exploded in front of me along with several buzzing whines of bullets. Erika shrieked. I flipped the safety off and went to work, blasting off a round at a nearby muzzle flash. The gates of hell cracked open, and all I could do was hope I took a few with me.

FORTY-FIVE

I shoved Erika down behind an open-ended pipe that stretched out across the front of the house. Bullets smacked and whined off of it, probing and seeking. I couldn't worry about Lane. He was busy ditching behind an old windmill. I lost sight of Brock behind the old Ford but could see a shadow and then his foot poked out. I took a shot, and Brock howled. Jake inside screamed in unison.

Another burst of tattered lightning came from the chicken coop. Erika stayed flat on her stomach. I inched toward the end of the pipe. I focused on the man hidden in the bush line. I caught a glimpse of a muzzle blast. I aimed, waiting for the next burst. When it came, I blasted a half dozen rounds downwind. The muzzle blasts ceased. Maybe I hit whoever was in there or maybe I hadn't. There was no more gunfire incoming from that position.

A shadow shifted by the barn. I let off a short burst of a half-dozen rounds. A scream could be heard and a man stumbled out. I shot off a triple-burst and the figure collapsed. Another shadow moved, running out. He lobbed something and I cringed. It happened too fast for me to react. A dull thump and a bloom of dirt erupted near Lane.

Lane disappeared in a cloud of dust. I heard a muffled scream and then silence.

"Lane!" I yelled.

Nothing but silence.

I saw a man by the chicken coop running away toward the fence line. I followed him with the sites on the M4, but he disappeared when the dust cloud floated across. I placed the muzzle over the pipe and searched. Nothing was there and no incoming shots.

I rose to a half-crouch. The compound fell silent. Jake wasn't screaming, Brock couldn't be heard. The part that bothered me was Lane lying near the old battered windmill. He wasn't moving. Erika grabbed my leg. Fear in her eyes. I suddenly felt sympathy for her and caressed her arm.

Somewhere a car could be heard. Its motor turned and a dust cloud boiled up on the distant road. Soon another car fired off and did the same. I poked around the corner of the Ford. Brock was gone. Long gone. After the explosion, Brock saw his chance and split right behind the other man hidden within the chicken coop.

I moved out looking for the two men I knew I had hit. Retracing the steps there was no one. Everyone had disappeared. I saw a splotch of blood, but there were no bodies lying around. I searched the chicken coop and found another smaller pool of blood and a Glock handgun. I scooped it up and tucked in the waistband of my trousers. I swore, cinched the M4 up, and went back to the house.

FORTY-SIX

Erika was kneeling by Lane. He rolled over on his back, blood seeping through his fingers while holding his intestines. The Glock fell from loose fingers.

"Jesus!" I whispered. Instantly, I jumped forward, squatted on my knees, and examined the wound. Lane became combative, and I grabbed his arm. "Damn it! Stop!"

"Jesus," Lane whispered hoarsely. "What the fuck?" The explosion had peppered him but the worst was the bulging intestine poking through his tattered shirt.

I took out my knife, flipped it open, and carefully cut away the tattered fabric before studying the injury. "Abdominal Evisceration," I said.

"What's that," he mumbled.

"Something I hate to say I'm familiar with." I looked over to Erika. "Go get my pack from inside." She nodded and took off at a run.

Lane fumbled inside his jacket. I grabbed his hand. "Wait," he croaked. He thumbed a number. The phone began dialing. "Going to help."

"I thought this was the last time."

"Exceptions have to be made this time."

I thought about bolting and running, but gave it a minute. Wincing in pain, Lane whispered into the phone. "I got a favor..." Lane winced. He handed the phone over to me with shaking fingers. "Take it."

I cautiously took the blood-stained phone and held it up to my ear. "Who's this?" The voice on the phone demanded.

"George and that's all your getting."

"That's a start," the Jersey-born voice replied. "How's Lane? It sounds like he's hurt."

I lowered the phone, looking at Lane. "Who the fuck is this, Lane?"

"Trust me...for once, you dumb-shit," he wheezed. "Get him to pick...you up."

"How is he?" The voice demanded.

"He'll be fine once he gets help," I said.

"He better be," the voice continued. "What the hell is going on?"

"Tell him you need a...ride," Lane whispered.

"We need a ride out," I repeated.

The Jersey voice didn't give me a chance to say anything further. "Madrid...you know that town? If you don't, get a fucking map. There's a place, an old junkyard just north of there. It ain't been used in years. Go there on a road marked County Road 9, got it?"

"Who is this?"

"You just be there." The line went dead. I looked at the phone and handed it back to Lane. He took it and smiled through thin lips. His skin color was pale and his breathing more labored. "He knows...what...to do," he gasped.

Erika ran back, clutching the pack to her chest. I grabbed it and shook it until it unrolled. I grabbed several packs of sterile pads, a morphine shot before quickly donning the surgical gloves. Ripping one pack of sterile pads open, I grabbed the sterile water solution and doused the pad down.

I picked up the syringe of morphine and popped the cap. Lane's eyes went wide. "Where the fuck you get that?"

"Mexico has a wide assortment of material," I said as I stabbed the needle in his leg and pressed the plunger. "In a second or two, you won't feel anything."

I set about my work, carefully sliding the wet pad under the bulging intestine. Lane quivered but the morphine was taking effect. He wasn't screaming anymore but lying back and breathing somewhat normally. Dousing another pad, I laid it across the top of the exposed bulge.

A lot of people make the wrong assumption that you got to push the intestines back inside the cavity. That is the worst thing anyone could do. The best thing one can do is leave the intestines hanging out. Patch it over to keep out the worst of the contaminants. The next step was to evac the patient to the nearest facility for proper medical attention.

I took up the black sharpie, leaned over, and scrawled an 'M' on Lane's forehead. At least the EMTs might understand that he had been dosed with morphine already.

I spent several minutes patching him up the best I could. The bleeding had slowed but that didn't mean he was out of the forest as yet. While I patched him up, he watched me through curious eyes. "You'd have made a good doctor."

"Maybe," I said. I tightened up the bindings. Lane winced and let out an exclamation of pain. "Sorry, boss," I adjusted the bindings. "You'll do fine, but it's going to be a long trip before we're done.

Lane passed out. If he survived for a bit longer, he'd have a chance.

I scrounged for zip ties in the kit, stood up, and went to the house with Erika in tow.

FORTY-SEVEN

I went back into the house. Jake was shaking. He had managed to move away to the corner of the living room. I walked over and slapped him. I rolled him over and zip-tied his legs and arms again for double strength in that he wasn't going to go anywhere.

He held up his arms trying to fend off anymore blows. "What're you going to do now? Kill me?"

I smiled. "No, Jake," I leaned back. "There's some real shit coming for you. You are so screwed."

Erika stood behind me. Jake looked pleadingly to her. "Erika, you of all people should understand?"

Erika shook her head. "You're not a good person like I thought."

"But I am," he whimpered. "I really am!" He pointed to the

kitchen. We got money....we can split it," he looked at me in the eyes. He was realizing his world, his plans were crumbling. "We can split it..." his voice trailed off.

"I could kill you, but I got other ideas, Jake." I dug out a crumpled cigarette from my pocket. I spent a moment and lit it. "This one time you can redeem yourself."

Jake saw a glimmer of hope. "How?"

"When the cops get here, you tell them what happened here. Tell them everything."

"Everything?"

I stood up walked back to the desk, and rummaged through the papers. Most of it was US Marshal's material. I found several with the information I needed. I folded the papers and stuffed them in my back pocket.

"What do you mean everything?" Whined Jake.

"Just what I mean. Look, to get in the program, you have to tell the truth no matter how bad. You have to tell them you killed, you embezzled, and you name it."

"That's not what Brock said."

"He lied."

"Why, why would he..."

"Because he had plans to kill you," I took Erika by her hand. "Just tell the truth, Jake." We stepped out into the porch. I made a quick check on Lane and found his vitals were stable.

"Did you lie to Jake?" Erika asked.

"I did."

"What'll happen?"

I took her hand again and we walked out of the compound. "A very good possibility he'll be married to the guy with the most cigarettes in a Federal prison about this time next year."

When we got to the Buick I felt a wave of nausea wash over

me. The events of the night were too much. I didn't want to think about the people I had shot. I tossed the bag into the back seat. I unslung the M4 and tossed it in on top of the bag. Erika came up and looked in the back. "Are you okay?"

I could've fallen over. "Yeah, let's just get going." I pointed out in the distance. Several strobing red and blue lights sparkled off in the distance. The cavalry was coming and before too long, there was going to be an army of cops flooding in and God knew who else.

"Are you okay though?"

"I'm fine, Erika!"

"I don't care about the money!" She yelled back, shaking her head. "I really don't, George! I was just hoping for some money to get out of New Mexico and this mess!"

I laughed. I hadn't laughed that hard in so long. It felt good. "I thought the same thing the first time!" I hobbled over to the passenger door, popped it open, and fell into the seat. I was still laughing.

She slid in behind the steering wheel, her long legs hit the gas and we spun away down the road. "Life isn't all about money, George."

FORTY-EIGHT

The overhead bell dinged and rattled as the door opened to the old thrift store. Erika went in first and I followed behind, limping through the doorway. The only other person in the store was an old woman with blue-tinged white hair perched behind the cash register. She lowered a battered Harlequin romance novel, gave us the stink eye for a minute or two before deciding we were harmless enough for her to go back to reading.

We made Madrid in good time. We stopped once back at the Zia RV and Motel park, where I gathered up my things, and took a few moments to clean up before hitting the road. It felt good to take a shower. It was better when Erika slipped in to shower with me. The pressure and stress of the night faded away, and we found comfort and solace in our gentle embrace and caress'.

Before heading to the meeting place with the mysterious Jersey man, Erika saw the second-hand shop and insisted we stop. I couldn't argue. I was too damn tired.

Dust floated silently across the sun-lit voids between the shelves and racks of old antique goods that hadn't been touched in months if not, years. Erika slid between the racks of clothing, began searching through the piles for clothing to fit both of us.

A rack nearby held a wide assortment of postcards, some old, others new, and all were labeled from New Mexico. I twirled the display slowly, eyeing the cards. I spotted one that appealed to me. *Ah, the ideas*, I mused. I took hold of the card showing Torrance County's borders. The card would fit in nicely with the plans I had in mind. I took it, and hobbled over to Erika at the counter and laid it down.

"May I borrow a pen?" I asked the blue-haired woman.

She looked down at the postcard then back to me. "You do plan on paying for that?"

"I do," I held out my hand.

She fumbled around under the register and produced a pen.

I took out a crumpled paper from my pocket. It was a report sheet listing where Logan and Amy lived in Montana. I laid it out and began scribbling a few lines on the back of the card. I carefully copied the address from the US Marshals papers. I just wished there had been a phone number listed. A phone call would've been so much easier. I thought for a moment then scribbled the words 'PW" in a spot that was close to Pinos Wells. Hopefully, Logan would be able to figure that out. I scribbled a note on the back, warning them.

"Is this a good idea?" Erika asked. She watched over my arm.

I finished jotting down the address. "They need a warning, Erika. I owe them that much."

"Enough to risk getting caught, possibly," she looked up to the old lady. "Maybe make things worse?"

"It's a risk. I jumbled everything up and ruined their lives." I added the finishing touches, added several stamps. "I should never have come back."

"But you did," she said.

"For all the wrong reasons."

"If you hadn't, they would've come for you and your friends anyway. Then, there's me. Where would I be right now?"

"Mail?" I handed the card over. My hard gaze didn't leave Erika's own brown eyes. She had a point. Either she'd be dead or in someone's hands for bad things.

Erika placed her hand over mine.

The old woman finished putting everything in the plastic bag. "Mailman comes around in about an hour. I can give it to him then."

I handed her the pen.

The bomb was set. It was up to Logan and Amy to figure out how to get out of harm's way. There was nothing more I could do or offer at this point.

I just hoped beyond hope the two of them would listen. I hoped they could forgive me.

EPILOGUE

Our Good Samaritan was some Jersey-born mob kinda guy. At least I suspected he'd been mob at one time in his life. He went by the name Wolf. I found the name fit him. We parked off a dirt road just outside the ghost town known as Waldo right by an abandoned junkyard on CR 9. For a ghost town, there wasn't much for the ghosts of old to stay in. The 'buildings' were nothing more than rotten adobe-bricked foundations melting back into the land.

The noon-time sun hung high over the surrounding mountains just as a Cadillac sedan roared up, and slid to a stop. The engine died and a giant stepped out from behind the steering wheel. He wore Bermuda shorts, flip flops, and a loose silk shirt covered in pink flamingos and palm fronds. You could've puked on it and it wouldn't have shown.

He removed the aviator sunglasses from his face, smiled thinly. "You George?"

I debated on grabbing the AR but thought better of it. "I am."

"Who's the skirt?" He asked referring to Erika.

"Erika," I replied. "She's with me."

He mumbled some words, walked back behind the Cadillac, opened the trunk, and reappeared with a little red gas can, the kind you buy from those cheap dollar store places. "Load up your shit."

We loaded up everything we had, which wasn't much. The last thing I put in was the AR after I removed the magazine and cleared the weapon.

"You got everything?" He asked.

"Out of the car? Sure," I answered.

He muddled over to the Buick, the sound of his sandals slapping the soles of his feet. He twisted the top off the can and began dousing the car over. He whistled a soft tune to himself, stepped back, and lit it up with an old zippo. The flames burst to life and the interior became embroiled in rolling flames and thick black smoke. Satisfied, he walked up like a giant admonishing two kids.

"When we get to where we're going, the rifle stays in the trunk," he said firmly.

I shrugged. "Sure thing."

"Any more guns?" He was reading my mind.

I looked at him in silence.

"If I gotta ask again, I'm leaving you two knuckleheads out here. I don't need this shit, not today," he said.

"A Glock," I answered.

He held out his massive paw. "Hand it over."

"Not a chance," I replied.

"You used it, right?"

"Had to," I lied.

He choked and grinned. "I'm assuming a few people got a few holes in them because of it. You get caught with it you'll burn because of forensics. It's elementary gangster shit one-oh-one. Get rid of the piece after you used it, so hand it over."

I took a deep breath, sighed, and nodded. I reached back and pulled out the Glock from my waistband. Wolf took it and tossed it in the truck. It wasn't a big deal. I still had my Taurus 66 and the Browning stuffed in my duffel bag. I wasn't going to tell him that.

"Okay," he said. "Let's get going before the cops get here."

We whisked away in an ocean of Frank Sinatra playing from the CD player. It was evident Wolf was partial to 'Ol Blue Eyes, which led me to further believe he had been mob-connected. No doubt about it. Ericka smiled but there was concern etched in her eyes. For the following hours, we drove through Santa Fe, the assorted jangled lines of casinos until we bypassed Española. We stopped once for gas, empty the bladders, and grab a few things from a run-down gas station at some pull-off in Pojoaque. By the bright light of the afternoon, we arrived at Lake Heron.

Wolf steered the Cadillac along the dirt road. For a couple of hours, he'd focused on the road, keeping a wary eye on the rearview mirror. Not a word was said unless he was whistling along with Frank Sinatra. He was prepared for this venture. I saw the bulge and black walnut handle on a dark-framed revolver, a .38 snub from the looks of it, jammed between his legs.

He handed over a key and pointed toward a small white over green cabin. We hardly exchanged a word but when he spoke, it was with a firm resolute tone.

"You don't move unless I know about it," he said. "I'll be checking in from time to time, and I better find you here, *capish*?"

"Understood," I answered.

He got out, popped the trunk, and helped pull Erika's bag out.

"I'm right down the road," he paused, pointing back down the road we came up on. "I'm in the first green cabin on the left. If you have any problems, any at all, you go there. He slammed the trunk lid shut on the Cadillac. "Other than that, I don't want to see you hanging around for social visits. We ain't friends, got it?"

Erika hitched her bag up higher on her shoulder. "Is there any way we can go to town?" She paused and looked around. "Which way is the closest town?"

"I already stocked the place up but in case," he shook a finger. "Back down the road, take a right at the T, then follow that to the blacktop, make a left, and to the main highway." He offered to take her bag, and we moved up the driveway, talking. "If you do go, send me a message," he paused. "Shit, I gotta burn phone for you to use." He set the bag down, dug around in his fanny-pack, and produced a pink flip phone. "Only text me, phone calls mean trouble, got it?"

I took hold of the phone. "Transportation?"

Wolf sighed. "I gotta answer everything, Jesus. Lane has a Jeep in the garage behind the cabin. The keys for it are hanging up beside the fridge." He paused and shook a meaty hand in front of my face. "Now, I'm telling you, if you so much as scratch that thing, I'm gonna put my foot up your ass."

"Why are you doing this then?" I asked.

Wolf craned his head, looking up through the trees, pondering his next words. "Lane saved my ass and I owe him big. I get a call I go do as I'm told."

"Loyal soldier kinda thing is it?"

He shrugged his large shoulders. "Any man, who throws me a lifeline as he did, deserves my loyalty."

"WITSEC?"

He went quiet for a moment contemplating his response, his nostrils flaring. "The less you know the better."

"So, you're in the program?"

"Look, this whole thing," he paused, opening his hands. "I don't know what you did, frankly I don't want to know, but I suspect," he pointed a thick finger at me. "This thing has to do with all that bullshit going on in Estancia and Los Lunas, right?"

I took a deep breath, sighed, and nodded.

"It's best you stay here and stay quiet. Any problems and I'll come running but it better be legit, not some 'run-for-pizza' kind of emergency either."

"We got it," Erika said. "Thank you, Mr. Wolf."

He turned away, the sound of sandals slapping, and got back in the Cadillac and drove away. I stood there a minute pondering on what to do. I looked over to Erika. I could think of plenty of things. For once, I was glad to be here. It wasn't the best of situations but it was better than the alternative.

Erika tugged on my arm. "C'mon, let's go."

I slung the duffel bag over my shoulder, winced when the strap rubbed a sore spot, and we walked up to the cabin. I handed Erika the keys and she popped the door open.

Like Lane, the cabin was spotless. Everything had a place and was meticulously dust-free. I set the bag down by the door. On the far wall was an entertainment center with a large television and a large array of DVDs and old paperback books. I had a feeling we'd become bored over time. I looked in the adjoining room where a large bed lay just in the line of sight. Thoughts of boredom vanished when I looked up to Erika who was admiring the kitchen layout.

"How long?" She asked. "How long do we stay here?"

I looked around the small living room. "Not sure. Once Lane recovers enough, we'll know what to do next. I'm sure Lane will know." I picked up an old copy of *People* magazine from the end table. Justin Bieber stared back. I grimaced. I didn't know Lane was into reading about celebrities. That was hard to imagine. "I hope it's soon, but I'm thinking we're going to head out."

"Head out? Where?"

"Corona."

Her face wore a mask of confusion. "Corona?"

"Your uncle? Pinos Wells?" I said.

"When?"

"I figure about a week."

"I have relatives down there," she smiled.

She opened the refrigerator and rummaged through the food within and came away with a small apple in one hand and a Budweiser beer in the other as a prize. "George," she said. "There's beer, do you want one?"

I shook my head. "I'll just take a coke if any is in there."

She looked up in surprise. "Just a coke?"

I stepped over to her, took the beer out of her hand, and set it carefully on the counter. "I don't think we need any of it."

I took up a can of Coke, pulled the sliding door to the deck open. I took a deep breath. A wave of weariness washed over me. I popped the can open and took in a deep drink.

Erika smiled. Her brown eyes were radiant. I reached up, brushing the strands of black hair away from her face. A long moment fell between us.

"This could be interesting, George," she smiled.

I took hold of her hand. Sometimes the lonely find each other stumbling in the fierce rage of night. I went back to watching the trees sway in the gentle breeze.

"Another thing...my name is James," I said. "James Hendricks."

Larry and Ava Williams are living the good life in Montana under the watchful eye of the US Marshals. That all changes when Larry receives a mysterious postcard from a friend from long ago. He warns them of imminent danger.

With only a single clue, Larry and Ava are forced to go on the run as wanted fugitives and return to New Mexico where it all began. They soon are sent spiraling into a maelstrom of deceit and violence.

Coming 2021

Moriarty, New Mexico is about as far as Logan Pierce got before the money and the El Camino gave out. He'd hoped for a clean start in life as a field mechanic working for any company willing to pay top dollar for his skills in the oil fields of West Texas. Low on funds and out of options, he begins a change of course in his mechanic career and takes a job as a technician at Duggan's Truck Stop.

The truck stop is a miniature city within a city that has all the luxuries for a home away from home feel for the over-the-road truck driver. Under it all, Logan discovers there is also a dark side which people claim is owned and operated by the Dixie Mafia. Then there is the persistent rumor that the Mafia is searching for a quarter million in missing cash.

The job was meant to be a temporary solution but that was before Amy Hauser entered the picture and presented him with additional problems. They want nothing more than to leave New Mexico for a new life, but then again…there's that rumor of the quarter million in missing mob cash.

And Logan just may well have discovered where it's hidden, but soon finds that some people want it more.

www.ingramcontent.com/pod-product-compliance
Lightning Source LLC
LaVergne TN
LVHW091130080826
845145LV00008B/2113
9781732428133